Tales of Khayr Presents
False Light

Story by Selvir Katich
Written by Ezra LC
Series & World Architect: Wes Al-Dhaher

Brotherhood of the Wolf

ISBN 978-1-965754-10-8

Tales of Khayr
Seattle, WA
talesofkhayr.com

False Light is part of the *Brotherhood of the Wolf* series.

Story by Selvir Katich. Written by Ezra LC.
Series created by Wes Al-Dhaher.

Publishing assistance by BookCrafters, Parker, Colorado.
www.bookcrafters.net

From the Publisher

Dear Reader,

Welcome to *False Light*, a 30,000-word novella that lives between Issues #1 and #2 of our *Brotherhood of the Wolf* graphic novel series.

When we began crafting *Brotherhood*, we knew there were stories within this world that couldn't fit within the panels of a comic. Some moments are too atmospheric, too inward, or too haunted. Prose lets us breathe in those shadows, to slow down and explore ambition, fear, and temptation in ways only the written word allows.

That's what *False Light* is. It isn't required reading for the graphic novels, but it deepens the journey. This story, architected by our Creative Director Selvir Katich and written by Ezra LC, draws you into the haunted Serbian frontier of the fifteenth-century Ottoman world. At its heart is Tahsin, a Janissary confronted not only by political intrigue and whispered superstition, but by his own illusions of caution and control.

Its central theme is one that speaks across centuries: *"A man's worth is no greater than the worth of his ambitions."* -Marcus Aurelius. In these pages, that truth is tested in a landscape where ambition can be divine or corrupt, luminous or false.

At Tales of Khayr, our mission is to tell stories that are both sophisticated and pulpy, classic narratives refracted through the lens of an Islamicate world. Whether you've come to *Brotherhood of the Wolf* through comics, games, or now prose, it's our privilege to share this world with you.

Thank you for joining us. May this interlude enrich the saga to come.

Wes Al-Dhaher
Publisher, Tales of Khayr

Prologue

CARDINAL JULIAN CESARINI was deep in the throes of research when a knock sounded at the laboratory door. There were few servants in the tower, and fewer still who might dare to knock at his door while he was so engaged. The knock came again, weaker, as if the knocker thought better of it but simply couldn't help himself.

"Nearly there," he muttered. "Nearly… there!"

He got his fingers around the thick, slippery vein—he could almost swear the thing writhed like a snake—and snipped it with the scissors in his other hand before pulling both from the body cavity, along with a fresh kidney.

He wiped his gore-slicked hands on a fresh, white linen and swept to the door, opening it to find one of the servants, head bowed at such an angle his back had taken up the rest of the burden, leaving the man nearly folded in half.

"What is it?" Cesarini demanded.

"There is someone here to see you, Lord Cardinal."

"To… see me?"

People came and went from the tower; soldiers, mercenaries, spies, and the sundry multitudes that went into making sure there were fresh meals to eat and fresh white linens to wipe his bloodied hands on, but on a whole Cesarini did not entertain there.

"Who is it?" he snapped.

The servant flinched and mumbled something that sounded like "Francovick," possibly because he mainly said it to the floor.

"Stand up and speak up."

"Stefan Branković."

Cesarini cast his eyes upwards, asking the Almighty for patience, at least enough to not have the whelp gutted and laid out on the table next to his other subject, tempting as the thought was. He glanced back at the table where his masterpiece lay, a thin sheet covering the corded muscle and reinforced bone. Having a… fallback to test some of the more delicate arcana on might not be a bad idea. But the Branković boy failing to return to his worthless father would only lead to more problems.

"Bring him to my chambers."

"Yes, Lord Cardinal."

Cesarini examined his nails, each a little crescent of dark blood. "Send a basin of water first."

* * *

Cesarini would have preferred the man wear a blindfold; even the crippled on the street had the decency to do so. It would have saved him the disgust of staring at the scarred, fleshed-over sockets in Stefan's face.

Still, once his attendant had left, it allowed Cesarini the luxury of not bothering to hide his expression. They were wholly alone. Though Cesarini vastly preferred others to do his fighting for him, in the event of some sort of altercation, he expected even he could best a blind man.

"Lord Cardinal, thank you for seeing me."

Cesarini felt his lip twitch in amusement at the choice of words. "Your father has been most accommodating and I would hardly be a man of God if I did not show you the same kindness."

Stefan was a fine specimen, but for those missing eyes. Cesarini wondered what the point of keeping a warrior's body was, once there was no hope of fighting again. He would make an excellent test subject. And who was to say Djuradj would blame him? The roads were less than safe these days, with bandits hiding behind every tree, not to mention the Ottomans. Cesarini dipped a quill in the inkwell on his desk and absentmindedly started sketching the man, splayed out on a table, skinless, those lovely muscle fibers exposed.

Stefan had been talking. "… me here to get to the bottom of it and if I can't, I'm to ask you to leave the tower."

The scratching of the quill paused, and Cesarini looked up from his half-finished sketch. "The bottom of what exactly?"

Stefan frowned. "Please do not insult me and my father by claiming ignorance. This tower may be a good distance from Ćuprija, but rumors travel at speed. Missing children, strange things sighted in the forest…"

Cesarini nearly had to bite his lip to stop from commenting on that language again.

"My father cares not if you choose to throw yourself into the dark arts, but he cannot allow you to do it here in his lands when it is affecting his people. What sort of ruler would he be?"

What sort, indeed? The sort who cowered in Hungary, espousing what a great leader he was while the heathen horde blinded his sons with hot pokers. Then he dared send one of the brats to hamper the very man working on something that might push them back?

Cesarini swallowed the words and forced a smile onto his lips, even if it was only for himself. "I respect your father's position—" He did not. "—and I respect you further for telling it to me plain." He absolutely did not.

Stefan bowed his head slightly. Cesarini picked up the quill and pressed the nib against the paper, harder than he needed to, scratching two black eyeholes into his sketch.

"While I will admit to… dabbling in alchemy, I cannot and will not take the blame for every peasant superstition, lost lamb, or Turkish attack happening out there. Missing children? You more than most know the cruelty of the Turks."

To his credit, the man didn't so much as flinch.

"You are aware of how they… *find* recruits for their army?" Cesarini continued. "Of course you are. I assure you, the Turks' hunger for young boys is… substantial."

Stefan shifted in his chair, the motion of a man who need only be told what he wanted to hear, and that would be that.

"You are a brave man, Stefan Branković, and I am sure God sees that as clearly as me." He smirked at the verbal jab, and at the thought that God would give a single shit about this worthless child spawned from a worthless father in this worthless, backwater country. "Your family has treated me well—" If one drafty tower in the vacant countryside could be considered as such. "—so I feel I can confide in you. I am close, so very close to something that can turn the tide against the Turks. Something that can not only drive them from the lands of God, but grant you some justice for the great injustice done upon you."

Stefan's lip twitched. "Justice won't bring my eyes back."

"Perhaps I can."

Stefan stiffened at that and spoke very slowly, the edge in his voice making Cesarini think—if only for a moment—that perhaps he should have kept a guard on this side of the door after all. "Do not presume to taunt me."

"I do no such thing. Through God, all things are possible, my child." He took a fresh piece of parchment and began scratching away at it. "And through Him, the faithful are rewarded for their faith and their… discretion."

Scratch, scratch, went the quill as he filled the page with the appropriate alchemical rituals.

"Can I…" Stefan's tongue flicked over his lips. "Can I really see again?"

4

There was nothing so delicious as watching a man fall over the edge into faith. *Blind faith*, you could say. Cesarini had to stifle a chuckle.

"I have faith you will. You will need to follow these rituals to the letter. Do you understand?"

"Yes," Stefan breathed.

"Good. Here." He extended the scroll, rolling his eyes as Stefan groped for it, then keeping a firm grip as the man tugged at it. "Can I expect you will explain the situation with the Turks to your father for me?"

"The… yes. Yes, of course. It's as you said—there is no depravity the infidels won't sink to."

Chapter One

"THERE IS NO DEPRAVITY THE DISBELIEVERS will not sink to, and make no mistake, Djuradj Branković consorts with Lord Hunyadi even as he kneels for the Sultan."

Tahsin nodded as he hurried along beside the quartermaster. He was still sore from morning training when he'd spent an hour slapping his palms against a stone until they bled, still sweaty from when an officer had decided to loom behind him as he fired his arquebus at the range, and still hungry from breakfast, when he'd been unable to choke down more than a few bites of lentil soup due to his nerves. He had foolishly expected more of a respite after the Battle of Varna, and had instead been immediately given a new, dangerous mission, and all simply because he'd been in the wrong place at the wrong time.

Never stand out, that was his motto, though he felt giving voice to said motto would make him stand out, so he mostly kept it to himself.

"I heard you distinguished yourself on the battlefield," the quartermaster was saying. "Heard you cut King Wadislav's head off and stuck it on a pike."

"Something like that," Tahsin mumbled. It was partially true, though at the time, King Wadislav had been pinned under a horse. And he'd been dead. And his head had mostly already been lopped off already by—

"Koja, there you are."

The giant—the very one who'd done the lopping—sat cross-legged, hands resting on his knees, the featureless metal mask he always wore giving less than nothing away. His massive axe—the very one that'd done the lopping—lay on the blanket next to him, blade gleaming in the early afternoon sun.

Koja remained silent for a long enough moment that Tahsin thought he might have been napping. A nap sounded wonderful, sounded considerably better than a lengthy ride to Morova to meet with a despot who was ostensibly a friend, or at least ostensibly not an enemy.

"Little Rabbit," the big man rumbled, armor creaking as he got to his feet, plucking up the axe as if it weighed nothing before slinging it over his back. "I half expected you would be hiding somewhere."

At that, the quartermaster hid a snicker. Tahsin suddenly considered the man might have been mocking him the entire time, and it sent a hot flash of irritation through him. He was a Janissary, an elite warrior, and it should have earned him some damn respect. At the very least, he'd been there distracting Wadislav when Koja had cut the man down; he'd been close enough to be splashed all over with his hot blood and smell it when the man's bowels released a final time. And what had this man been doing? Counting sacks of grain?

Tahsin held himself as upright as he could, though next to the giant he may as well have been a child. "I have been given a task by the Agha, and I intend to see it through. Though there has been a change of plans. Before Kluv, we will be heading south to Ravnica Monastery to meet—"

"My task has not changed," Koja said. "So it matters little to me where we go or who we meet. I leave that to you."

"Then come along already," the quartermaster said. "Your task, his task, I've my own tasks to attend as well. No idea why I'm meant to see you off personally, though I suppose that's what happens when there's a hero in the mix." He hurried in the direction of the stables.

"Don't you mean two?" Tahsin muttered as they followed, keeping to himself any comment on the man's job giving him the ability to count.

A noise emanated from beneath Koja's mask, and Tahsin decided he would think of it as a chuckle, regardless of any real evidence backing that up.

His mood brightened when he found a group of Sipahi waiting for them at the stables, loaded with gear for the road. His mood subsequently darkened when he realized their numbers were barely a half-dozen, and then turned positively black when a tall man strode straight for him and looked him up and down with an expression one might give a rather unimpressive turd.

"You two are who we've been waiting for? I should have your feet whipped." His voice matched his face, which was to say it was imperious, harsh, and altogether certain it was the best voice to ever grace a stable. His dark hair likewise matched his dark armor, both gleaming, both lustrous, and both well-kept. It was either the armor of someone who saw little battle, or someone wealthy enough to maintain its appearance through repair or outright replacement.

"I had—" Tahsin's voice creaked as he withered under the gaze of the man and the equally unimpressed Sipahi behind him. "I had duties to attend to," he finished. "You and your men are here to support my mission as—"

The man took a furious step forward, looming over Tahsin. "My men obey me, not sniveling rats in ill-fitting Janissary uniforms." He lifted an arm and made to drive his finger into Tahsin's chest. "*You* will not—"

He stopped dead, staring down at his finger, which had never made it to the target; instead, his wrist had been caught by Koja. "How—how *dare* you touch me!?" he spluttered, going to yank his hand back and struggling at it; Koja's meaty palm encircled the man's wrist effortlessly.

"Striking a commanding officer will lead to much worse than a foot whipping," Koja intoned. "I'm doing you a favor."

"Release me!" the man shrieked, dropping his free hand to the sword on his hip. The Sipahi rustled, a few of them doing the same, and all of them straightening, tensing.

"Koja," Tahsin said, placing a hand on the big man's arm. "Release him."

Koja did so, and the man yanked his arm back, rubbing at his wrist.

Tahsin bowed his head. "I believe we have gotten off on the wrong foot. While this mission may not be what *any* of us intended, it is what we must do, at the behest of the Agha, and for the glory of Allah. I am Tahsin Katabasis, Çavuş of the Janissary corps," he said, straightening his back. "And this is Koja Hizir, Serdengeçti of the Sublime Porte."

The man's gaze slid to Koja. "What is an elite like yourself doing with a coward who whips other cowards to the frontline?"

"He has no need to whip me there."

"Who do we have the pleasure of—" Tahsin searched a moment for the right words. "—working with?"

The man lifted his chin, which was a feat considering its current height. "Cem Demirci of House Demirci, Sipahi of Thessaloniki."

"Demirci?" Koja asked. "Your father is Emre?"

"Yes," Cem said tightly. "What of it?"

Koja gave no response which only served to irritate Cem further.

"Cavalry," Tahsin said, grasping at anything he could get his hands on as he glanced over the man's shoulder to the massive warhorse, wearing matching armor, with a matching dark mane, and, somehow, a matching, unimpressed expression. "That's perfect. We will defer to your expertise when it comes to combat—if it comes to combat, that is. I will handle boring things such as diplomacy, logistics, and… such." He got the impression if he let Cem or Koja handle diplomacy for the course of half a conversation, things would indeed devolve into combat. "Inshallah, it will be an easy ride there and an easier ride back."

Cem snorted, and his horse did the same. "We shall see."

Chapter Two

"Do you know who you are talking to!?" Cem roared from atop his horse—Şafak, Tahsin had learned, and he'd also learned the man cared more for his horse than any of his companions.

Of course, even if it hadn't already been clear, it would have become so as Cem all but foamed at the mouth as he screeched at two dozen heavily armed soldiers wearing black mail, their tunics embroidered with Orthodox crosses. They blocked the road, weapons not yet in hand, but certainly not far from them either.

"Weren't you supposed to handle diplomacy?" Koja asked from his horse beside Tahsin.

"Yes, dammit," Tahsin grumbled, edging his horse forward and lifting a hand in peace. "Thank you, Cem, I'm certain they do not know who you are, nor the rest of us. I am—"

"We know who you are," the lead soldier grunted, working a gob of spit from his throat, to his mouth, then to the muddy track below before continuing. "You're here to see Despot Branković."

"No, we are here to see—" Tahsin frowned. "How did you know?"

"Come," the soldier murmured. "He's waiting for you."

Tahsin made what he hoped was a conciliatory gesture, but he could feel it coming across limp-wristed before he was even halfway through. The man spat again, turned on his heel, and gestured for his men to escort Tahsin's group through the streets of Ćuprija to the looming stone edifice of Ravinica Monastery.

Due to an unfortunate bottleneck on the road, Tahsin found himself riding alongside Cem. The man had not warmed to him during the weeklong trek to Morova. If anything, he'd done the opposite. It seemed the yoke of Tahsin's command, such as it barely was, chafed him worse than anything imaginable.

Cem caught him looking and sneered; Tahsin had to admit, as much as he hated the man, he had a very good sneer. When Tahsin attempted the expression, it never came out quite right. Perhaps he just didn't have the bone structure for it. For that matter, as much as he hated the man, he had very good bone structure as well, the sort a sculptor might make a whole era out of.

"I know I should not be surprised to see you simper for those beneath you, but I am all the same. Do you have no pride?"

It took Tahsin a moment to register that Cem was talking to him. "Eh?" was all he managed to muster.

"You let a common soldier boss you around. Do you strive for nothing? What does your heart beat for if not to make something of yourself? Is that not what sets us apart from the animals?"

Tahsin blinked at him, trying to determine if he actually wanted a response, or simply to talk more. Cem answered for him.

"A man's worth is no greater than that of his ambitions." Cem spat, though it was hardly as impressive as the gob the lowly soldier had managed. "Let me explain that in terms you might understand with some time; you have no ambitions, therefore, you have no worth. And I do not respect you."

With that, he gave his horse the heels, the horse gave a derisive snort in Tahsin's direction, and the infuriating Sipahi rode ahead, leaving Tahsin mercifully alone for the remainder of the ride.

While the town would hardly be mistaken for a bastion of civilization, there seemed to be some sort of festive atmosphere, with flags flapping, walls mostly washed, and those people he did see out and about wore clothes that both approached clean and approached colorful, though their moods did not exactly match their dress. They spoke in hushed tones and turned suspicious eyes on him and his entourage. He turned in his saddle to look about.

"Feast of Ascension," Koja grunted.

"Eh?"

"The day Jesus Christ ascended to heaven."

"Oh." Tahsin wrinkled his nose as if he'd smelled something foul. "Christianity."

"If they don't kill us, we can expect some good food."

"Is that… likely to happen?"

"I doubt Djuradj would settle for anything less than a feast on the day of Ascension."

"Not the food!" Tahsin hissed. "The other thing. The *killing.*"

"Oh." Koja shrugged. "If it were me, I'd have done it before we got to town. But you never know."

* * *

Tahsin had spent the entire ride to Morova thinking he couldn't ask for worse traveling companions—one, a taciturn giant, the other, a lit cannon fuse, ready to explode at any moment.

That was before he'd sat at a Christian feast, in a Christian city, on a Christian holy day , feeling dozens of eyes on him as the sweat and grime of the road—for they had arrived without time to wash—set him further apart from the finely dressed attendees of the feast. Despot Djuradj Branković had waved to them from across the room, acknowledging their presence, but nothing else. He sat to Tahsin's right, at the head of a massive table. Tahsin sat between Cem and Koja, about halfway down. If the gazes of those closer to the despot were displeased, those of the nobles to Tahsin's left were downright acid.

Conversation filled the room—it was a celebration after all. Though there was a sort of bubble around the three of them where the conversation still flowed, it was just of a hushed variety, the type you might have while discussing a plot against someone's life while that person was in the room, for example.

Tahsin met the eyes of a woman sitting across from him, flanked by her husband. He attempted a winning smile and nodded his head.

"This is… spectacular. The food, that is. Not the occasion. I mean—" He looked to Koja, who gave a shake of his big head so perceptible it could have been used to signal a cavalry charge from a mile off. "That is—an occasion to celebrate. Ascension." He coughed, took a sip of water to cover it, did it slightly too fast, and then coughed again, so violently that Koja lifted a hand to slap his back. Thankfully Tahsin waved him off before the damage could be done.

Tahsin decided to keep his focus on his own plate, not the way Koja lifted his mask to chew loudly beneath it, not the way Cem let out a little huff of disgust at the way Tahsin held his utensils, and certainly not on the soldier leaning in and whispering in Djuradj's ear, and the resultant way the man's eyes flicked over Tahsin's group, then away to the man sitting at his right hand.

Tahsin hadn't looked too closely at him before, though now he did. He was maybe perhaps thirty, and wore fine green clothes. Wrapped tightly around his head and tied at the back was a matching green blindfold. Djuradj leaned towards him, speaking out of the corner of his mouth, his eyes never leaving Tahsin's group.

"Grgur," Koja said around a mouthful of chicken.

"Eh?"

He swallowed. "Grgur."

He hadn't misheard, but it did little to elucidate things. "His name?"

"Yes. Djuradj's son." Koja reached for more chicken.

"Oh yes," Cem said. "I recall that mess. After Djuradj fled to Hungary, Grgur was appointed governor in his stead. But the sneaky bastard was conspiring with his father all the while, so the Sultan ordered him blinded, along with his younger brother Stefan."

Tahsin shuddered. He understood the practice—a blind man could hardly rule—but it bordered on barbaric, especially extending the punishment to the man's younger brother.

"Your knowledge is extensive," Tahsin said, sensing an opportunity to, if not get on the man's good side, at least slip ever so slightly further from his bad one.

"I had an education," was the only reply.

Tahsin tilted his head and looked to Koja, who was reaching for another drumstick to add to the little pile of picked-clean bones already on his plate. "You attended the same school as our illustrious Cem? Why didn't you tell me?"

"Didn't know all that," Koja said.

"You didn't? Then how do you know the man's name?"

"I blinded him," Koja said.

The choked wheeze Tahsin made could have easily been heard across the table were it not obscured by the chewing, smacking, and popping as the drumstick went up under Koja's expressionless mask for a few brief seconds before joining the others on the plate, picked bare to the bone.

Chapter Three

"Do you think he knows?" Tahsin asked as the three of them waited in a room, not exactly prisoners, but not exactly free to leave.

Cem's men were at the stables, and Tahsin had no doubt Djuradj had more outside the door, in addition to the two who flanked it from this side.

"He knows," Koja said.

"How? It's not like the man could see you."

Koja turned the impassive mask towards him. "He saw me before I blinded him."

"Oh. Right—of course." He was babbling, which he tended to do when he was nervous, which he tended to be when he sat waiting to see if he was about to be blinded or worse.

"Try not to piss yourself," Cem said. "You stink of fear as it is."

"You're taking this surprisingly quietly," Tahsin snapped. "The great Cem, waiting in an empty room for an hour, would have thought you'd have fought your way out of here single-handedly by now."

Cem gave him an even icier glare than usual. "There are worse things than being blinded—"

"So you think he's going to blind us too!"

"—and I will make sure you experience them if you don't shut your yapping mouth."

"He's coming," Koja said.

Cem stiffened and Tahsin cringed, then was surprised to find Koja's hand on his shoulder in what he could only assume was meant to be a comforting gesture.

"Remember your mission," Koja said, as if remembering it would keep a hot poker from searing out his eye sockets.

"Right," Tahsin squeaked, because he didn't really know what else to say. "Right."

The door swung open, and Djuradj swept inside, followed by two more guards. To Tahsin's surprise, there was nary a hot poker in sight, nor three burlap sacks, nor a single hooded executioner.

"Friends!" Djuradj boomed, spreading his arms and hurrying over to sit across from the three of them at a wide table. He was a broad man with a thick black beard. "Apologies for the delay, you know how it is after a feast, everyone always wants to stay and gossip the night away."

Tahsin did not know, and he had difficulty believing Koja had been to many feasts.

Cem's gaze was no less withering for being directed at a man who could likely have them beheaded with a single flippant gesture. "If it was only gossip, there was no reason to keep us wait—"

"We all know what it's like," Tahsin said quickly and loudly, shooting him a glance. "You have to practice *diplomacy*—" He made sure to hold Cem's gaze. "—or you don't know *what* might happen."

"Quite. Now," Djuradj said, "what can I do for the Sultan of the Turks? I'm afraid I don't have another son around for you to disfigure."

Tahsin gave perhaps the weakest smile of his life in response to that, and he had given some weak ones.

"I find diplomacy works best when all the cards are on

the table, no?" Djuradj flicked his eyes over Koja. "We all must do what we must to protect our own after all. I want to protect my people and my family, so I would love to expedite you from my lands as soon as possible. What will that require?"

Tahsin was so surprised—so *pleasantly* surprised at that— that he could barely work his tongue into function. "Ah—ah, very gracious of you, very gracious and of course we wish the same, well, you know what I mean that is…" He was babbling again. "Yes, the thing is, the Agha has sent us for… boys. The battle—the Battle of Varna—was… costly, and the army is in need. You understand."

"Of course. The Sultan needs a strong army. The man has many enemies," said Djuradj.

"Heh. Yes." Tahsin couldn't help but feel the other shoe was about to drop, but he pushed on. What else was he to do? "So, if you can provide us with your tax ledgers—just to see the numbers, you see, not that we don't trust what you tell us, just that—well, it's official… business and all. So it's all above the table."

He rapped on said table for emphasis, the sound echoing dully in the mostly empty room. Merciful Allah, how long had he been talking for? It seemed like an eternity had passed since his companions had said a word, and, while a few minutes ago he'd been praying for that very thing, now that it had happened he wasn't quite so sure it was for the best.

"There is," Djuradj began, and Tahsin's heart sank, "just one matter that needs to be attended to first."

Tahsin gulped and hoped it wasn't audible. "A… matter?"

Djuradj tapped the table with a well-manicured finger. "Two actually. There is a wolf terrorizing the villages. Has killed a good number of people, some in broad daylight if the rumors are to be believed, dragged right from town. I want you to find it and kill it."

"Are we huntsmen now?" Cem muttered.

"We will see it done," Tahsin said quickly, speaking over him. "And the other matter?"

"There have been disappearances of late. Children, you see, and not ones headed to your Sultan."

Tahsin gave a watery chuckle that matched the feeling in his bowels. "Is… that is, the children have not been taken by the wolf?"

"Unless the wolf has been climbing in windows to take them as they sleep, no."

"Ah."

Djuradj gave a lengthy sigh. "If the matter is not dealt with, you'll have trouble finding many at all to bring back as soldiers. The people have suffered much, and I fear if this is not dealt with, there may be outright rioting at the thought of more children being… levied."

"Yes…" Tahsin said. "That would be…not good."

Djuradj slapped the table, sudden enough that Tahsin jumped. "Good! We're in agreement then. You kill the beast, figure out who is behind these disappearances, deal with them, and I will have those ledgers waiting." He glanced to Koja again and gave Tahsin a smile that was utterly devoid of mirth. "I think that's a fair trade, don't you?"

"Yes," Tahsin said quickly, nodding so violently it made him dizzy. "Yes, quite fair."

"I suggest you start in the village of Senje. It's where the last man was killed from what I'm told."

Chapter Four

"I AM A SIPAHI WARRIOR. I fought at Varna and killed a Transylvanian banneret, and you expect me to go tromping through the woods looking for a *wolf*?"

Tahsin sighed. He'd expected Cem wouldn't like the plan, which was why he'd waited until they'd nearly arrived in Senje to tell him—Cem and his men would hire a local hunter and begin the search for the beast while he and Koja spoke with the locals about the missing children. If anything, Tahsin thought he was doing the man a favor by letting him kill something rather than talk to someone.

"Is it beyond your capabilities?" Koja asked before Tahsin could muster a response.

Cem sputtered with rage. "Beyond my—you must be joking."

"Have you heard him do so?" Tahsin asked.

"Djuradj is a *vassal*. We do not answer to him. We should ride back to Sultan Murad, gather an army, then return and put the man and his crippled family to the sword."

Tahsin pinched the bridge of his nose. "The army is recovering from the Battle of Varna, or have you forgotten that is the whole reason we're here? We aren't going to war over one man dragging his heels while the whole of Christendom is waiting for any sign of weakness from us."

"You're one to speak of weakness," Cem snarled, "after you rolled over for him like a bitch in heat."

Tahsin was fairly sure dogs didn't roll over in such a situation, but he felt it wasn't the time for a correction. "It galled me equally, I'm sure. I'd be much happier to simply demand the ledgers, but since it's the three of us and your men against a despot, one of the richest men in the Balkans, I think it would end with us being the ones who disappear. Would you prefer the task of speaking with grieving mothers? Or can you handle this?"

Cem gave an almighty sneer. "When I return with the beast's pelt to find you've failed to make progress, we'll deal with the peasants *my* way." He gave his horse the heels and thundered past into the village, followed by his warriors.

Tahsin let out another sigh, though this was more the sound he made slipping into a warm bath; Cem's absence did just as much to relax him. The sensation was short-lived.

"Do you think we should have kept some of his men with us?" he asked, turning to Koja.

"We will be in the village. I expect there will be little I cannot handle."

"Inshallah," Tahsin muttered, and nudged his horse down the rise into the village below.

* * *

Tahsin's hope for a quick and easy task died well before he and Koja reached the center of town. It was immediately apparent they were not welcome here, and though he was certain Cem had made an impression, the man couldn't have infuriated every single inhabitant. On second thought, Tahsin had no doubt he *could* if he spoke to them, but the man simply couldn't have had the time.

The villagers stared at the pair of them with fear, anger, and outright disgust. Plenty of doors were slammed, plenty of spit was spat, and Tahsin was considering Cem's suggestion of outright invasion by the time Koja spoke.

"Perhaps we will find someone more accommodating there."

Tahsin followed his gaze to a squat, windowless building with a faded sign hanging from the thatched roof. "A tavern? Don't tell me you want a drink?"

"A smart man would turn none away, even the likes of us. Especially if we're paying."

Tahsin sucked his teeth. "It's hardly a good look to be seen in such a place."

Koja gave a slow glance around the empty street. "Do you think anyone here is going to care?"

"Good point."

The interior was even less appealing than the outside. It was dim, smoky, and smelled strongly of sweat, or something close to it, despite there being only a single table of patrons inside. They looked up from their drinks and dice, fixing him with gazes that could only be described as predatory, though as Koja stepped through behind him, ducking under the doorframe, they went back to their game, only shooting them the occasional glance.

Tahsin strode up to a short bar behind which a tall woman stood, wiping her hands on a rag. She had pale, delicate skin, though her arms were shaped by hard work. A few strands of blonde hair peeked from beneath her dark headscarf. She looked him up and down then did the same to Koja, albeit slightly slower, though that could have been simply because there was considerably more up and down to him.

"What'll you have?"

"Hm? Oh! Nothing for me," Tahsin said quickly. "Nothing for us. We didn't come here for that."

"What did you come here for then?"

"Ah—" Tahsin tried his best to peer around her. "Perhaps we could speak with your husband?"

"You're welcome to."

"Thank you—"

She pointed out the door. "Cemetery is that way."

"Oh—I'm—I'm sorry to hear that," Tahsin said.

She let out a sigh Tahsin was all too familiar with—the sigh of someone whose patience was growing thin. "I'm Jelena and this is my place, so whatever you wished to speak with my husband about, you can say it to me."

"Ah," Tahsin said, slowly sinking onto a stool. An empty tankard sat on the bar nearby and he nudged it away. "Well. Is that…" He was still searching for the correct word—decorous didn't seem quite right—when Koja spoke.

"We heard a wolf killed a man here recently."

Jelena flinched, then went very still. "It was not a wolf."

Tahsin perked up. "You know who was killed? That's wonderful, who—"

"It was my brother, Teodor."

Tahsin opened his mouth, then closed it. "I am… so very sorry to hear that."

Jelena nodded. "So was I. Same way I was sorry when—" Her voice broke. "—when my boy went missing. Nobody did anything then either."

Tahsin's heart sank for her. Without even realizing it, he'd reached for her hand. He thought better of it halfway there and turned the gesture into an awkward lifting of the finger. "Perhaps—do you serve anything without alcohol in it? We would like to ask you a few questions if that's alright."

She nodded slowly. "What's your name?"

"I am Tahsin, and this is Koja."

"Well, Tahsin and Koja, I don't know you and while I'm usually fond of newcomers willing to spend money, something tells me you aren't about to become regulars."

Tahsin gave a weak chuckle, unsure where she was going.

"I'll tell you under two conditions. One, I need you to

believe me." Her eyes flashed. "No matter how ridiculous the story sounds."

Tahsin glanced at Koja, who, as usual, gave nothing away. He couldn't imagine a reason why the woman would lie, so he felt there was no harm in agreeing. "Of course."

"Great." Jelena nodded at the group playing dice in the corner. "And I want you to get rid of them."

Tahsin turned. Five men sat at a table, some of them large, most of them dirty, and all of them within arm's reach of a weapon, either a knife on their person, or in the case of two, sheathed curved swords leaning against a nearby table.

"Get… rid of them?" Tahsin asked.

Jelena nodded. "And make sure they don't come back."

* * *

Cem wasn't going to come back empty-handed. The thought of that whinging little cretin Tahsin and the pleasure it would no doubt give him was more than enough motivation. He was certain he'd return in no time, wolf pelt in hand, to find that the weasel and the giant had made no progress on the missing children, leaving Cem to solve that problem too.

He just had to figure out how to find the beast. His men knew better than to offer unsolicited advice, musings, or words of any kind, unlike his new companions. It simply wouldn't do to ask his underlings for advice. For the first time, he wished he had taken his brothers up on their many offers of hunting trips. The entire concept was beneath him—tromping through the woods, hunting a feckless beast which had no chance against his superior intellect?

He was a Sipahi warrior, the son of the Sanjak Bey of Thesselonika and destined for greatness that would shake the world. He needed no help. He took command and was decisive.

Cem stared out at the woods for another few minutes before speaking. "Yilmaz."

His scout rode forward to stop alongside him. They were on a rise overlooking the village below, high enough to give an unobstructed view of the dense forest that stretched out all around it.

"Sir."

Cem stopped himself from looking to the others where they waited, still mounted, and, more importantly, out of earshot. "You are an able hunter, are you not?"

Yilmaz nodded. "Able enough, sir. Often easier to trap my own food than pack it out on a long scout."

Cem nodded. He would have preferred a simple "yes" without a whole boring history of the man, but he said nothing. "And what do you know of wolves?"

Yilmaz scratched his head. "They'll usually only attack people as a last resort. Have to be real hungry. If it is as they say and a wolf's been doing all this, I'd say it's gotten a taste for it. A man-eater, and it likely won't stop until someone stops it."

It was harder this time, as the man rambled on as if he were being paid by the word, but Cem resisted the urge to snap. "I meant how to hunt them. Where might we find the beast?"

"Ah." The scratching had shifted to below his chin, in a vigorous enough manner that Cem made the mental note to give the man a wider berth around camp. He seemed to have some sort of skin condition which Cem had no interest in catching. "I'd say we find a hunter in town and ask what they know. Anyone been hunting these woods for years could point us in the right direction."

Cem had been worried he'd say that. He'd been so irritated he'd ridden straight through town to the other side without a plan. Going back now would make him look like a fool, and he wondered how he could save face in front of his men. The alternative was to send them fumbling around in the woods with no clue where to begin, which would also make him look a fool.

"After we're pointed in the right direction, it's a matter of drawing the wolves out," Yilmaz said.

"Wolves? There is more than one?"

"Well, they hunt in packs don't they?"

It sounded vaguely like something Cem had heard at some point in his life, but trifling details in the natural world held about as much interest for him as… well, as something else boring and unimportant. "Of course," he snapped. "So we'll kill them all. Even better to bring back a dozen trophies."

"Of course, sir."

"What about this bait?" Cem looked over his men. "Selim could do it I imagine, he looks like easy prey."

"Oh." Yilmaz turned in his saddle, then turned back. "Ah, best bait usually isn't a man, the wolves might not come out. Sheep, goat, something like that. We get a general idea of where to go, stake the thing out there, make sure we're downwind, get up in a tree and take them with bows when they come for it."

Cem wheeled his horse back around. "Right. Back to town. There's still plenty of daylight to get this trap set."

Chapter Five

KOJA TOWERED OVER THE TABLE OF MEN. He was used to towering over people, and expected he'd continue to do so even after they inevitably stood and made things messy. Still, there was no reason to not make an attempt.

"Now what's this big bastard want?" a dark-haired man asked. Koja pegged him as the leader of the group.

"Maybe he wants to join us," another offered.

"Ain't enough room at the table," whined a third, "and you know I hate pullin two round tables together."

"Good thing I was fuckin' jokin' then, isn't it?"

"Oh."

"You need to leave," Koja said.

"Eh? Says fuckin who?" sneered the leader.

Koja pointed back to the bar where Jelena and Tahsin both watched. Jelena said something out of the corner of her mouth and Tahsin winced.

"If she wants us gone she can come right over here—" The man slapped his lap. "—sit down, and ask me herself, all nice like."

"She has asked you to leave. Leave."

The atmosphere changed at that, any hint of joviality vanishing like smoke in the wind. Chairs which were previously leaned back now had all four feet solidly on the floor, and slouched positions straightened, hands coming to rest on weapons.

"Look here," one of them said, standing, then craning his neck to look up at Koja, poking him in the chest with a finger, "why don't you—"

Koja clamped a meaty hand over his face, lifted him, and smashed his head against the table, tilting the whole thing over, spraying dice, fruit wine, and stew all over the floor as the other men shouted and stood, chairs clattering to the ground as weapons were drawn.

"That'll be the last mistake—urgh!" The dark-haired man's words cut off in a pained groan as Koja gave the upended table a mighty kick, sending it shooting across the floor and taking the man's legs out from under him.

A man scrabbled for his sword, turning to catch Koja's fist straight to the chest. The air left his lungs with a great oof, along with a decent amount of spit. He crashed into another table, slid from it to bounce off a chair to the floor, where he lay wheezing for air and clutching his chest.

Crack! Something caught Koja across the side of his mask. He turned to find a man lifting a cudgel for another blow. As it came down, Koja caught it, stopping it dead. He yanked, meaning to tear it free and found the man's wrist attached to it with a leather lanyard. He spun, the man screeching as he was lifted from his feet and then howling as his shoulder was freed from its socket with a horrible *pop*. The howl increased in pitch as Koja released the club, sending the man crashing into a wall where he fell in an unconscious heap, finally going silent.

The last man was already backing away, and when Koja turned to him, he dropped his knife, turned and sprinted for the door, leaving a faint trail of liquid and the distinct smell of urine.

A familiar scrape made Koja turn—it was the sound of steel leaving leather, a sound he'd heard many, many times, a sound which changed things. The leader stood there, nose bloodied and hair wild, holding a drawn blade.

"You'll pay for that you monster!"

He dashed forward, making it clear which way he'd swing before his arm even went back. Koja stepped within his reach, drove a palm into his chest even as his other hand clamped around the man's wrist. With a twist, he shattered it, eliciting a high-pitched shriek of pain, the sword dropping into Koja's waiting hand. He could almost hear the roar of the crowd, and though he hated them, their cheers woke something inside him.

The man dropped to his knees and Koja had already flipped the sword around, point down over his shoulder. The man stared up at him, eyes wet and horrified as Koja drove the blade down.

"Koja!"

He stopped, the point scraping a fine red line against the man's shoulder where it had pierced his shirt and little else. He turned.

Tahsin stood, hand outstretched. Jelena looked on horrified, her hands clasped over her mouth. "That's enough."

Koja stared down at the man, who, like his companion, had pissed himself. He looked considerably younger blubbering on his knees, little more than a brat and barely out of his teens.

"Do not come back," Koja said, laying the blade against a chair.

The man nodded frantically, clutching his ruined wrist to his chest, snot and tears trickling over his lips.

"If anything happens to Jelena…"

He stomped the blade with a booted foot and it shattered. Koja dropped the hilt next to him. "Go."

* * *

It took a few awkward minutes for the sniveling, half-dazed

men to collect their things and limp from the tavern. Tahsin spent it with a strained smile on his face, hoping Koja's… enthusiasm hadn't cost them their most promising resource. She had asked for him to *make* them leave after all, hadn't she? And there had been no meaningful bloodshed, though the giant had been a split-second away from killing that last man.

Tahsin eyed him now, for the thousandth time wondering why he bothered. The mask was as expressionless as ever, the only hint of difference a slight dent where the cudgel had struck him. Though perhaps there was another difference—Koja breathed a little quicker, sat a little stiffer, though he'd said nothing after returning to the bar.

As the door swung shut behind the last of the group, Tahsin fortified his smile and turned it on Jelena who had recovered from her horror, though he noticed she kept a little more distance from Koja.

"Well," Tahsin said brightly. "There you have it."

"There…" A frown pinched her brow. "And my dining room looks like a herd of wild boars just ran through."

"Apologies," Koja murmured.

"No no," Jelena said quickly. "I'm not—thank you. Really. I asked you to. I just need to—I need to get it tidied is all, before dinner. It may come as a surprise after all this, but I try to run a welcoming establishment."

"Yet you serve alcohol?" The words slipped out before Tahsin could stop himself.

Jelena pressed her lips together. "Koja, may I get you something to eat?"

After the briefest of pauses, the big man nodded.

Tahsin's stomach rumbled. "I could—"

Jelena rummaged under the bar and came up with a rag, pressing it into Tahsin's hands. "You can start cleaning up. I'll join you in a moment. We can talk then."

Tahsin felt vaguely irritated with the woman, who had asked them to risk themselves—even if it had mainly been

Koja—getting rid of a violent gang. Now she was making him clean like some housewife? He shot Koja a glance, looking for any sort of sympathy, but the big man simply stared ahead in silence.

"Go on," Jelena said, disappearing into the kitchen behind the bar. "I'll be right out. And you'll have a hot meal after, I give you my word." She lifted her eyebrows and gave him a smile that, for reasons he couldn't quite explain, sent a rush of heat to his ears.

She joined him a few minutes later with a broom, sweeping up a shattered bowl as Tahsin rubbed the rag at a bit of blood on the floor. "So," he grunted, trying it again with his knuckles pressed to the rag. "Can we talk?"

"And spoil the enjoyment of watching you clean? You might be the first man I've seen scrub a floor on his knees."

Tahsin glanced up to find her leaned against the broom, looking down on him with a smirk. "You mock me."

"Hardly. It's appreciated."

"Well," he grunted again, giving up on that particular stain and heaving himself to his feet. "You can show your appreciation by explaining what in the fires of hell is going on around here."

Her expression fell. "What indeed." She extended the broom to him. "Here."

Tahsin looked at her, incredulous. "Woman, you intend to make me sweep while you watch?"

"No, just hold it a moment."

Tahsin watched, transfixed as she untied her headscarf, revealing a tight bun of ashen blonde hair which she undid, letting it fall well past her shoulders as she combed her fingers through it.

She caught him staring and a smile tugged at her lips. "Sorry."

"That's—no need for an apology," he said quickly, looking down to push around some broken porcelain with the broom.

"Sometimes I just need to let it down and give myself a good scratch."

Tahsin nodded, chancing another glance at her. To his relief, she was in the process of winding it back up into a bun. "So."

"So," she said, replacing her headscarf and extending her hand for the broom. "I think you've done enough. Put your feet up."

"That's alright," Tahsin said. "I don't mind helping."

She seemed surprised but pleased as he went about picking up the scattered chairs and tables.

"I'm sorry," she said. "It's… more difficult than I thought it would be. A few weeks ago I was telling anyone who would listen, begging anyone to listen but…"

"Take your time," he said. However long it took, surely this would be better than scouring the town for a friendly face. And hers really was friendly—it was… vibrant, every expression reaching from her lips all the way up to her eyebrows, throwing her whole self into whatever emotion she was feeling.

"They found my brother in the woods a month back. Said it was a wolf attack."

"He was mauled?" Tahsin asked gently.

"Yes—no. It—" She looked down, fiddling with the broomstick. "I have lived here my whole life. I have seen a sheep after a wolf's been at it, seen a man's leg with a dog bite. My brother was not killed by wolves, not killed by anything even resembling a wolf."

Tahsin remained silent. He knew he should perhaps say something, but decided saying nothing at all would be better than saying the wrong thing. Instead he busied himself with wiping a table clean of a red smear. His rag caught on something and he leaned down, feeling his stomach twist as he realized it was a tooth embedded in the wood.

He glanced at Jelena, who was still looking down, gathering

her words. Tahsin sidled around the table to block her view and pinched the tooth between two fingers, trying to work it from the wood.

Jelena blew out a long breath. "What a mess I am. I prayed for someone to listen and God has delivered me just that and I suddenly can't speak."

"As I said, please take your time," Tahsin said, rocking the tooth back and forth.

"I have taken enough. What killed my brother… what took my son…" With one last deep breath, she looked up at him, her eyes piercing. "It was unnatural. Something evil. And it is still out there."

Chapter Six

THE GOAT TROTTED AROUND THE CLEARING. It tugged at a bit of nettle, uprooting it from the ground before chewing, swallowing, and looking directly up to where Cem perched in a tree before letting out a prolonged, human-like shriek, which startled him so much he nearly lost his grip.

"Aaaaaaahhhhhh!"

"What in Allah's name—is the thing possessed?" Cem pointed as Yilmaz, sitting on the next branch over, bow in hand, gave him a strange look. "Did you not hear that? It sounded like a man. We should kill it swiftly before it draws a djinn here."

"Ah… it is a sound some goats make, beyim. Not uncommon." Yilmaz winced—as he should—at Cem's withering gaze. "I wouldn't expect you to have troubled yourself with the calls of livestock. But I promise you, nothing unnatural about it."

The goat let out the awful sound once again, and it was Cem's turn to wince. "It is a horrendous noise."

"You get used to it. At any rate, the noise is good for us as it will draw the wolves, though—" He lowered his tone. "We should keep talking to a minimum, as we don't want the beasts to hear us."

That suited Cem just fine. He'd had quite enough barnyard

education for one day. He shifted on the branch, searching for a more comfortable position and then shifted again, sending a few leaves fluttering to the forest floor below. One leg had fallen asleep, and it took a mighty effort to unfold it and stretch it without dislodging himself and going the way of the leaves. How in God's name did the other man stay so still? Cem supposed the scout was used to scrunching up in a tree and whiling the time away. He hadn't seen so much as a rustle from the trees across the clearing, so it seemed his other men were just as used to the discomfort.

After a time, his other leg began to ache, and he went through the whole process in reverse, sending another shower of leaves down. All through it, Yilmaz remained perfectly still but for his head, which shifted ever so slightly towards Cem every time he moved, as if the man considered looking at him but thought better of it.

Merciful Allah, he was bored. This was hunting? He'd never felt warmer towards his younger self. Even as a child he'd been wise beyond his years, and was wiser still now. He would slay these wolves, succeed in this ass-stain of a mission and be on to bigger and better things. He would show his brother Firuz—he would show them all. He would shine brighter than the sun, and they would do nothing but shield their eyes from his splendor…

"Aaaaaaaaahhhh!"

Cem started from a half-doze and slipped from his branch, jerking to a halt, heart pounding and neck choking as Yilmaz grabbed him about the collar and, with a mighty heave, hauled him back into place.

"Are you alright?"

Cem made an irritated noise in the back of his throat and regretted it, opting to keep quiet and massage his windpipe, answering with a curt nod. He'd dropped his bow, and it had clattered down through the branches, bounced, and ended up in the clearing. The goat skipped over, sniffed it, and immediately began chewing on the string. Cem let out a sigh, which hurt his throat, and settled back onto the branch, shifting his weight to the other leg once again.

Yilmaz touched his arm, and Cem readied a blistering reprisal at the presumption, but before he could, the scout nodded down. Cem followed his gaze. The goat had stopped chewing. It stood, very still, head cocked, listening, one wet eye fixed on the underbrush.

* * *

"My boy was different in the last weeks before he disappeared. He was always so bright and full of life." To Tahsin's surprise, Jelena's voice grew stronger. "Something changed him. He grew distant, quiet. Pale and thin and bruised all over. Would stare at the edge of the forest for hours. He loved playing there and it's never really been dangerous around here—the village is downhill, it's easy to find your way back. The smoke can be seen above the trees, and he'd never go far."

Tahsin said nothing. Now that she was talking, he intended to let her do so, uninterrupted.

"My brother and I didn't know what else to do—we forbade him from going back. The fit he threw when we told him." She shook her head. "You would have thought him possessed. But he eventually calmed, and after a few days he actually seemed better. Was eating more, was talking more." She held a hand to her mouth, pausing, then lowered it. "We thought it was over. And then he was gone. The whole village went looking of course, but could find nothing. Barely a week later, my brother was gone too. I thought it really was a wolf until I saw his body. That's when I knew whatever had taken my boy had killed him too, killed him for searching."

Jelena took a deep, shuddering breath. "He was covered in bites. Not wolf bites, they were far too small. They looked like… God protect me, they looked like the bites of a child."

Tahsin frowned. "A… child?"

Jelena managed a grim smile. "I doubt you've much experience with children and wet nurses, have you?" He had not, and she could see that. "I've been bit by an infant and even a bratty toddler. Leaves a very particular mark, a ring of teeth. Nothing like a wolf or a dog. My brother was covered in them. Dozens and dozens."

Tahsin looked to Koja. The big man gave the slightest shake of his head; he had no idea.

"That isn't all," Jelena continued.

"Merciful Allah," Tahsin whispered. "There's more?"

"You remember I told you my son was bruised?"

"Yes…" Tahsin said slowly.

"I didn't make the connection until I saw my brother." She took a deep breath. "The bruises on my boy were bites. Not enough to break the skin, not enough to leave teeth marks, but enough to bruise. Whatever killed my brother was—" She swallowed, looking sick. "Mouthing him. Nibbling at him."

Tahsin turned to Koja. "Have you ever heard of such a thing?"

The mask slowly turned from side to side, glinting in the firelight. "I have not. But…" Tahsin did not like the sound of that one bit. "There are… things out there that defy the natural world. I have seen them with my own eyes."

The hesitance in the giant's voice was not doing wonders for Tahsin's confidence. Whatever out there could make Koja nervous, he had no interest in meeting. He wiped a hand over his mouth, trying to muster a semblance of leadership.

The door crashed open and he jumped, turning from the table they shared. Cem strode directly across the floor towards them, followed by his dwarfish retainer, Vuk, a pygmy goat trailing the man on a lead.

"Aaaaahhhhhhh!" the beast shrieked.

Everyone but Cem winced. He loomed over the table, looking very pleased with himself. "While you've been sitting around having warm milk and honey like a babe, I have discovered something very important. The creature we seek—"

"It's not a wolf," Tahsin said. "We know."

Cem closed his mouth, swallowing back what looked like a throat-straining amount of rage and started again. "Very well. Did you know we seek not one beast but—"

"Many," Koja grunted. "We know."

Tahsin could actually see Cem's shoulders slump as all the verve went out of him. On second glance, the man looked out of sorts—his face was scratched and his normally perfect hair had a few snarled leaves twisted in it.

"How?" was all he managed to say, sitting heavily at the table.

Tahsin nodded to Jelena. "We asked."

"Oh."

After Tahsin caught him up, Cem did the same, finally explaining the goat, which had hopped up on a nearby table and stood there, turning in a circle for no apparent reason other than the enjoyment of it.

"The goat caught wind of the pack minutes before it arrived. We didn't catch sight, but we did wound one. Yilmaz fired an arrow into the bushes and got lucky." He threw a thumb back at the goat, whose head perked up. "You think that thing can shriek? You've never heard anything like these creatures. It was getting dark, so we couldn't follow, though they left clear tracks."

He paused, as if expecting another interruption. When none came, he continued, gratified, recovering some of his haughty tone. "The tracks looked like those of a barefoot child."

Chapter Seven

TAHSIN WAS STARTING TO THINK that Cem had a point about the locals, not that he planned to admit it to the man. Jelena had put them up in rooms and suggested a nearby stable for their horses. The plan—such as it was—had been to split up into a few groups and find anyone with knowledge of what lurked in the forest. Jelena had pointed them in the direction of a few other townsfolk who had lost children, and there was a smattering of grieving families with their own wolf-related losses.

Only, no one was the slightest bit interested in talking. At first, Tahsin had thought it was because they were Turks, though even a Muslim family who had recently lost a young man to a 'wolf attack' had turned him away, despite him offering money for their story.

Upon meeting back at Jelena's tavern for a quick lunch of fresh bread and some hard cheese, he found his companions had fared little better. Tahsin half-listened as he craned his neck. They were far from the only patrons, and a serving girl flitted between tables, though he had yet to spot Jelena. For that, he was partially thankful; he didn't want to relay only failures to the woman.

"Has this been a sufficient enough waste of time for you?" Cem demanded. "Or do you still expect your vaunted diplomacy to yield results?"

"We cannot start beating information out of people," Tahsin sighed. "We are meant to help these people, not terrorize them. I expect any stepping out of line will get back to Djuradj and I do not think we would like the result."

"Bah," Cem said, dismissing the argument with a sharp gesture. "Djuradj is the Sultan's dog and he is wasting our time on a fool's errand. The man is a Despot. If these villagers are so important to him, he would have his own people investigate the killings in force."

"Yet he gave us the task," Koja rumbled.

Tahsin frowned. "Clearly something more is happening."

"And my point is, Djuradj knows more than he's letting on," Cem insisted. "Mark my words, he's getting something out of this and it isn't a bunch of happy peasants."

Koja leaned forward. "Cem may be on the right track." He lowered his voice. "Were any of you followed today?"

"Followed?" Tahsin said. "No?"

"I was," Koja said. "Since leaving here this morning, a man shadowed me. Don't look—he's sitting in the corner even now."

Cem's head snapped around and Tahsin turned in time to see a thin man start, stand, and bolt from the tavern. Cem went hot on his heels, shouting for him to stop.

Koja let out a weary sigh as he stood. "Come. If we want anything left to question, we should make haste."

Tahsin was pleased to find that Cem had already caught the man, barely a street away. He was less pleased to see that the man wore monk's robes and was bleeding profusely from the nose, and even less pleased that more than one person had stopped and were staring at the commotion.

"Why are you following us?" Cem roared, slapping the man across the cheek. He held him by the collar, his back against a building.

The street wasn't exactly bustling, but nor was Cem making the slightest attempt to keep quiet—the last thing they needed was a mob of peasants surrounding them and asking why a group of Ottomans was beating a holy man, or worse, to have someone call the town guard.

"Down here," Tahsin said, gesturing Cem towards an alley. "Come on, get out of sight."

With a snarl, Cem hauled the whining man from the wall and shoved him into the alley, sending him stumbling to the ground in a heap. He collected himself, cupping his nose, and when he looked back, Tahsin was sure the sight didn't please him—Cem, glowering down with Tahsin beside him, and the massive form of Koja behind them, arms crossed and blocking the alley.

Cem took a step forward, and the man cringed. "Please," he whined, "please, I meant no harm, I was only doing what I was told."

Tahsin placed a hand on Cem's shoulder and the man immediately twisted away as if he'd been smeared with shit. "Don't touch me," he spat, though he did stop.

"Who are you?" Tahsin asked, ignoring him. "And who sent you to spy on us?"

"Radomir," he replied, dumping a cupped hand of blood on the ground before placing it back under his nose. "I am a steward for Lord Branković."

"Djuradj sent you?" Tahsin asked, confused.

"No, the other Lord Branković."

"Grgur," Koja said sagely. "Perhaps he plans revenge on me."

"Ah, for blinding him," Cem said.

"Yes."

"No!" Radomir said, pushing himself to his feet and finally giving up on his nose, which trickled a thin stream of blood down over his lips. "Stefan!"

"Oh," Koja said.

Radomir glared at the big man, then considering his situation, thought better of it. He straightened up to his full height, licked a bit of blood off his lips, and spread his hands. "May I speak?"

"It's what I've been waiting for," Cem growled.

"Yes," Tahsin said, mustering what patience he could, which, at this point was not very much at all. "Of course."

"Thank you," Radomir said, straightening up and sniffing. "I meant no ill-will towards you. I was simply sent to offer you an invitation but first I was to see what you were about."

"An invitation? To what?" Tahsin asked.

Before he could respond, a rapid set of approaching footsteps sent Tahsin and the rest turning. Vuk entered the mouth of the alley, breathing hard, still holding the lead which was still connected to the goat, which ambled in after him.

"Sorry, beyim," he panted.

Cem made a disgusted noise, waved his hand, and turned back to Radomir. "You were say—"

"Aaaaahhhhhhh!"

Tahsin jumped at the goat's shriek and was immediately embarrassed; merciful Allah, he was a Janissary. It wasn't his fault his nerves were shot after a week of dealing with… all this.

"What I was saying," Radomir said, looking down his nose at Tahsin now, "was that Lord Branković wants to see you."

"Djuradj'?" Vuk asked, hand propped on the goat as he caught his breath.

"No!" Radomir shouted, losing all pretense of control. "Stefan Branković wishes to see you at Ravanica Monastery. You are expected this evening. May I leave?"

Koja glanced at Tahsin, who nodded for him to step aside. Cem sneered as Radomir dusted himself off and walked away with his head held high, albeit with a bit of a limp and a lot of drying blood down his front.

"What the devil is his problem?" Vuk asked, patting the goat. "I only just asked."

"He's a prick," Tahsin said, glancing at Cem, who still

glared after the man, looking like he wanted to throttle him. "A raging prick."

* * *

"Ah, friend Radomir," Tahsin said as the man greeted them that evening at the gates of the monastery looking much better, but for some bruising around his nose. "It's good to see you well."

Radomir snorted, winced, then gingerly put a hand to his nose. "Lord Branković—*Stefan*—awaits you in his laboratory."

"Lead the way," Tahsin said. They'd discovered nothing of interest for the remainder of the day and had decided to search the forest next, albeit not until the following morning.

Radomir led them briskly through the monastery grounds where the group weathered the usual disgusted glances. So much for earning some public sentiment by hunting this 'wolf.'

The laboratory was a squat building set away from the main structure behind a beautifully appointed garden. Inside was a vast, well-lit space. Rows and rows of bookshelves covered the walls and long tables were set with beakers, pipettes, glass flasks, and all manner of tools Tahsin couldn't begin to guess at the use of.

Stefan Branković turned from one of the tables as the group entered. He had the same strong build as his brother and likewise wore a blindfold. "Ah, friends!" he said as they entered, setting a beaker in a little holder and hurrying to greet them. As he walked, he swerved around a footstool effortlessly before stopping in front of the group. "I have heard about you. Tahsin, the Janissary, Cem, the Sipahi, and you must be Koja, the giant." He faced each in turn, despite the fact the blindfold completely covered his eyes. "Radomir, you may leave us."

"But—"

Stefan waved a hand. "It's perfectly fine. They mean me no harm. I would see it if they did." He chuckled. "Please, come, come, find a seat where you can."

"What—what did you want to see us for?" Tahsin asked.

"Forget that," Cem snapped. "How can you see with that thing on? You were blinded with hot pokers, were you not?"

It took a considerable amount of Tahsin's dwindling willpower to not slap a palm into his own face.

Stefan smiled faintly, turning his head to Koja. "So I was. And let me tell you, your friend did a thorough job. For years I could see nothing. Living in absolute darkness… it is a fate I would wish on no man, not even my worst enemy. But, I have been blessed."

As he spoke, Tahsin noticed the faintest glow coming from behind the blindfold where his eye sockets would be.

"I didn't see you at the Feast of Ascension," Tahsin said.

"I was away in the south gathering materials." He waved a lazy hand around the lab. "The alchemical processes that allowed me to restore my sight were complex and required… exotic ingredients."

"Black magic," Cem spat.

Stefan chuckled. "A common misconception. Divinity created this world and all in it, did it not? I simply use the natural tools and forces of this world that have been put here for man to rule over." He pulled a stool out from under a lab table and sat. He moved like a man who could see, and Tahsin had no idea how it could be a trick. "I heard you've been hunting near Senje, looking for the wolf."

"It is no wolf," Cem snapped.

At this, Stefan stiffened slightly, though Tahsin wondered if anyone else saw it. "With respect, you are mistaken. It is a wolf. I must ask that you let me and my men handle it— with respect, I cannot have you tromping about the woods and destroying the delicate balance of plants and animals. I require things from these woods for my continued research."

"With respect to you," Tahsin said slowly. "Your father has given us this task."

"Yes," Stefan said, pressing his lips into a tight line. "I am aware of that. It would be best if this conversation remains between us. My proposition is as such—you simply give me a week and I will have the beast. I'll even let you deliver its head to my father so you can take the credit for it."

"I told you," Cem began. "It is—"

"That's enough," Tahsin said, just managing not to flinch under Cem's withering gaze. He'd pay for it later, but he didn't want to give Stefan any more information than he already had. "Your deal is acceptable."

Cem was sputtering with barely controlled rage, but it at least kept the man silent as Tahsin shook Stefan's hand and they took their leave.

Cem rounded on him as soon as they stepped out of the lab. "If you ever speak to me that way again—"

Tahsin swallowed his fear, ignoring the man. He turned to Koja. "Did you see how Stefan reacted?"

"Are you—are you ignoring me?" Cem demanded.

Koja nodded slowly. "He didn't like what Cem said."

"If you dare—wait," Cem said. "What? What are you talking about?"

Tahsin glanced back at the lab. "Stefan knows it's not a wolf."

Chapter Eight

TAHSIN'S BRAVADO LEFT THE MOMENT the others suggested he be the one to sneak into Stefan's lab.

"I am much too large for sneaking," Koja said. He glanced at Cem. "And…"

"A Sipahi warrior does not skulk about in the shadows," Cem sniffed. "It brings me no shame to admit I am not skilled when it comes to the trade of thieves and murderers."

"So you see," Koja said, slapping one massive hand down on Tahsin's shoulder, probably hard enough to bruise. "It has to be you, Little Rabbit."

"Vuk can accompany you," Cem offered.

"The… *dwarf?*"

"They gave a braying ass a Janissary's uniform, why would a dwarf not be good enough to be my retainer? Besides, his natural size makes him difficult to see."

"He's just short," Tahsin said, exasperated. "I think he's broader than I am!"

Cem flattened his hand and lowered it towards the ground. "Men do not look down at the dirt—they stare forward at the horizon."

"The Despot's *guards* will be looking every which way!" Tahsin said. "I don't think they are worrying about their ambitions as they patrol the monastery grounds at night."

Cem scoffed. "Spoken like someone with no ambitions—leaders think of their next great step at all times."

* * *

"Who'll watch the goat?" Vuk asked. "She's smart, chewed her way out of the wagon once already. Been squirmy since we got here, no idea why."

"Why'd you bring the thing?" Tahsin whispered. They had ridden ahead, while Vuk brought a small wagon to resupply the larger group back in Senje for their eventual return.

"She noticed whatever was out there before Yilmaz did, and that's not something I see often. Thought she might be useful. Didn't want someone to cook her while we was gone."

"Cem and I will watch the beast and the wagon," Koja said. "And we'll have the horses ready… just in case."

Vuk put his hands on his hips and spat. "Right. Any killin?" For some reason, he looked at Tahsin as he said it, in a manner that Tahsin did not care for one bit.

"No," Cem said, to Tahsin's relief. "At least, not if you can avoid it."

"No, no killing at all," Tahsin said. "Of any kind! Do you know what would happen to us if we were caught?"

"I won't be caught," Vuk said, which reassured Tahsin until he continued. "Not alive anyways."

"That's—" Tahsin gritted his teeth.

"You will be fine," Koja said. "The lab is well away from the main building. Keep your lanterns low when you're inside and nobody will ever know you were there."

"Good luck," Cem said wryly.

Tahsin cursed, flipped up the dark hood of his cloak and hurried off after Vuk, who was hustling around the corner of the stables, surprisingly quick. Tahsin could still hear Cem's voice fading as he rounded the corner. "Men of ambition don't need luck, of course…"

Then it was mercifully silent but for the sounds of night. Vuk took them on a wide circuit around the shadowy monastery grounds, and, though Tahsin could see some distant lanterns bobbing in the night as guards patrolled, they were few and far between enough that he allowed himself some hope they wouldn't be caught and skewered before the hour was out.

Vuk lived up to his reputation—the man was all but silent, making Tahsin's own quick footsteps as he followed seem painfully loud. Still, they made it to the garden without incident and were swiftly through. Vuk halted them at the edge, peering out over the dark grounds.

"Do you think anyone is inside?" Tahsin whispered, back pressed against a hedge.

"Can't see any light beneath the door, but could just be a good door. Any windows?"

Tahsin thought back to the visit. "Skylights was all. I think."

Vuk grunted. "Probably safe then. You want to go first?"

"Uh—if the door is locked—"

Vuk snorted. "Only joking. Quick now."

With that, he scampered across the last thirty feet to the dark side of the laboratory building. They would be fully exposed if anyone came by, without an alcove or pillar of any kind to hide behind, but it was pitch black behind the gardens; Tahsin got the impression Stefan's lab was meant to be out of the way of any normal visitors.

He caught the faintest scrape of metal on metal and then the lock clicked open. Vuk slipped through first, holding the door, and Tahsin followed. It shut behind him with a soft *click*.

Inside was even darker that the garden, though faint light came through the skylights overhead. Vuk reached into his cloak and drew out a finger lantern, holding it close to his chest before lighting it, keeping his body between it and the skylights.

"Where to?" he asked.

Tahsin had no idea where to start—there were hundreds of books on the shelves and it would be pointless to search them. Likewise, he had seen a half dozen lab benches and tables filled with notes. He could hardly read them all, and that was assuming he'd even understand any of it. But Stefan had been in the middle of some sort of experiment or research when they had arrived, and starting there seemed as good a place as any.

"This way," he said, heading off in the dim light and attempting to retrace his steps.

It went poorly. He remembered a distinctive glass distillation device on the bench Stefan had worked at, and he'd checked three tables already without finding it.

"Can we have some more light?" he whispered.

"More light there is, more risk we'll be seen. You'd be surprised what a glow there'll be even through the skylights."

Tahsin muttered a curse under his breath. He didn't want to be here all night, as that seemed a good way to get caught as well—who knew if Stefan might return for a late-night experiment?

"A little more at least, I can barely see my own nose in this."

Vuk turned up his lantern and Tahsin blinked away spots. It was still dim, but enough to get his bearings. He gestured, and Vuk followed as he doubled back across the room to the desk Stefan had sat at earlier. He scanned it for anything useful, having no real idea what that would even look like. He couldn't take something, as Stefan would no doubt notice immediately. While the lab might have been somewhat cluttered, everything was still clearly in its place and organized.

Tahsin flipped quickly through a small notebook, finding only the same rows of gibberish words in increasingly smaller sizes, starting huge and ending up so small he'd need a magnifying glass to read them. He had no idea what it meant. He carefully placed the notebook where he'd found it and cast around for anything else.

"Anything?" Vuk asked. "We best not hang around too long."

"Not yet," Tahsin said. "Just—let's check the bookshelves."

"You're in charge."

They hurried over to the wall of shelves, and Tahsin noticed for the first time there was a plush chair, footstool, and a little table tucked away in the corner. On the table next to the chair was a book.

"Here, bring the light," he said, kneeling and flipping the book open on the footstool. He quickly paged through it, met on each spread with a sketch of some fantastical, horrible creature and a page of text describing it. Some even had detailed drawings of the creatures after being dissected.

"Hay Allah! " Vuk exclaimed, peering over his shoulder. "What is that?"

"Some sort of… bestiary, I suppose. Though it's describing things I've never heard of, let alone seen."

"And do you think our beast from the woods is in there?"

Tahsin nodded slowly. "I do. But which? We can't take the book, especially since it wasn't even put back on the shelf. Something tells me Stefan doesn't entertain visitors here, he'd suspect us immediately.

"Here," Vuk said. "Take the lamp." He handed it over, swapping it for the book, which he closed, then placed on its spine against the footstool.

"What are you—"

Vuk let the book fall open, checked the page, then did it again; the book opened to the same page. He gestured for Tahsin to lower the lamp. "Chances are this is what he's been reading."

Tahsin peered at the page, his eyes going wide. "I think this is it." He scanned each line, mouth moving as he whispered the words to himself, taking a scant few minutes before closing the book and replacing it where they'd found it.

"Well done," he whispered.

Vuk seemed surprised at the praise. "Um… thank you."

Tahsin chuckled. "Unused to hearing praise from your master, I assume."

"Ah, he's not a bad sort once you get to know him…" He gave Tahsin a toothy grin. "He's even worse."

Tahsin let out a hoarse laugh, then clapped his hand over his mouth as he turned the lamp down.

"Time to leave," Vuk said, waving for him to hand it back over. "Let's go."

Tahsin nodded and followed him back across the lab, feeling rather pleased with himself, right up until the moment his shin hit a footstool, sending him tripping, arms flailing into a nearby table. He smashed a number of glass receptacles under his arms and chest, shards pricking through his clothes, and sent more to the floor where they shattered loudly, one even erupting in a little green puff of flame and filling the air with a chemical tang.

"What the—come on, come on!" Vuk said, hauling him back to his feet and taking off like a shot. Tahsin limped after him. Vuk had already snuffed the lantern and had the door open, one arm spinning like a windmill as he waved Tahsin through. He shoved it shut after him. "No point relocking it, they'll know we were there. Quick, back through the garden!"

Tahsin said nothing, he just followed. Every moment they hustled back through the dark hedges, he expected to hear a shout, followed by torchlight, but none came; they made it back to the opposite side of the monastery without seeing a single guard.

Panting, wet with chemicals, and covered in cuts—some of which were beginning to burn from said chemicals—Tahsin arrived at the wagon just behind Vuk. Cem and Koja leaned against the back, the goat's head poking out between the two of them.

"What happened?" Koja asked.

Tahsin waved away the question, trying to catch his

breath. His lungs were burning and seemed to get worse every moment.

"What is that smell?" Cem asked, recoiling and lifting a hand to his nose.

"I—" Tahsin rasped.

Vuk pointed. "You are smoking."

Tahsin looked down, eyes watering, and found that yes, he was indeed giving off faint wisps of chemical smoke. He drew in a breath to say something, which turned out to be a very big mistake, as it felt like huffing hot embers directly into his lungs. He let out a pained gurgle, dropped to his knees, keeled directly forward, and everything went dark.

Chapter Nine

TAHSIN WAS WARM. Comfortable, wrapped up in blankets. A woman was humming nearby, a soft, wordless tune that was vaguely familiar. The sound warmed him as much as the light on his face. He felt he could lie there peacefully forever—

A loud bang snapped open his eyes, and he shot upright in bed, wincing at a mottled chemical burn that covered his chest, along with dozens of cuts and scrapes, a few deep enough that they'd been stitched. He was so surprised at the state of himself, it took him another moment to wonder where his shirt had gone and where he was.

He turned and found Jelena staring at him. "Tahsin! Be careful."

Tahsin snatched the sheet up and covered himself, looking away from her, and warding her off with one hand. "Ah— where is my shirt?" The words scratched his lungs like shards of glass.

"That one was… unsalvageable."

Another bang at the door made her jump. "Wake up you wretch!" Cem called. "We've waited long enough."

Koja's muffled voice came through next. "It will do us no good to wake him if he's in no state to talk."

"I'm—" He'd attempted to call out that he was awake, but the words caught in a croak. "Clothes, please, Jelena."

"Of course—of course." She handed him a folded shirt, hesitated, then nodded and turned for the door. "I'll send them in and be on my way."

"No," Tahsin croaked. "Stay."

She turned back and his cheeks heated. He'd dropped the sheet and began to stuff his arms in the shirt, though he was stiff, and struggling somewhat to do so.

"Here," Jelena said, coming over. "Let me help."

Before he could protest—and perhaps for the best, as every word took considerable effort—she leaned down and helped him get his arms through the shirt, swiftly buttoning the front. Her fingers were quick and sure, and the brush of her knuckle against his bare chest sent a thrill through him, though it quickly faded as the door banged open and Cem strode through, followed by Koja.

He made a face at the scene. "What debauchery is this?"

"None," Jelena said. "I was helping him dress."

Tahsin surreptitiously checked and thanked Allah for the fact that his pants remained on. "Paper and a pen, please. Talking is hard."

"Are you alright?" Koja asked, a surprising note of concern in his voice.

Tahsin nodded, gratefully taking a cup of water from Jelena and swallowing a few cool mouthfuls. She exited the room, then returned with paper and a pen, which Tahsin took, twisting around to begin scribbling on the bedside table.

"What's this?" Cem asked. "Must you keep us in suspense?"

"Quiet," Koja said, peering down as Tahsin worked. "Let him finish."

After a few minutes, Tahsin set the pen down and slumped back into bed, handing the page to Koja. "That is what Stefan has been reading about." He took another sip of water as Jelena crowded in along with Cem, all three reading what Tahsin had last night before copying the most important parts down, word for word.

The Fae Harvesters

The Fae Harvesters are small, malevolent beings that look like grotesque, twisted children. These creatures prey on children. They always choose one who is lonely and overlooked—someone yearning for friendship, desperate for escape.

The Harvesters are happy to welcome them.

The games begin—long, bright days filled with joy and play. Hours vanish in fields and forests, filled with laughter and strange songs. Each day stretches longer than the last. At first, the child returns in the afternoon. Then, it's dusk. Eventually, they come home after nightfall—pale, exhausted, but smiling.

And then one day they don't return at all.

Other notes:

Adults slain by Harvesters are savaged, but not eaten. Flesh is ripped and mauled, but ultimately not consumed. Telltale signs of a Harvester attack show many small bites all over the body, with the neck often bearing the worst wounds.

Children under the Harvester's spell grow pale, weak, and distracted. They will often lash out, sometimes violently, if kept from the forest.

Jelena's covered her mouth in horror as she finished reading and Koja set the paper down. Even Cem looked slightly uneasy.

"You wrote this from memory?" he asked.

Tahsin nodded. "I often am called upon to copy letters or to write down a dictation. I suppose I have a good memory. Everything there is directly from the book. I couldn't memorize the entire page in the time we had, but I tried to take down the most important things."

"Impressive," Koja said. "Truly."

Cem plucked the paper back up, scanning it. "Unfortunately,

there is nothing here that tells us where to find the beasts or how to kill them."

"I don't remember that information from the page," Tahsin admitted. "I don't think there was anything there about that. But I could be wrong."

"We know they are in the forest," Jelena said, her voice shaking with rage. "And I can tell you without a doubt, this is what happened to my boy. Exactly what happened."

"The forest is enormous," Cem said. "We could search for years and not find this lair or whatever it is, and I for one have goals I will see completed before I'm an old man."

Tahsin nodded. "Cem is right."

Cem threw his hands up. "It's simply—wait, what?"

"We need more men to search the forest, which means we need Despot Branković to aid us. We need to take him proof that there is something more out there than a few hungry wolves. Surely the man will not let it stand. These… things are killing his people."

"What proof do we have?" Koja mused. "I do not fault your logic, but from his perspective, this sounds like the ravings of madmen."

He was only too right. Perhaps they could collect more testimony from the villages, even others than Senje, but it would take time. Djuradj could easily brush it all off as peasant superstition.

"I… have an idea," Jelena said. They turned as she wiped her tear-stained cheeks, took a deep breath, and stood tall. "We could dig up my brother."

Tahsin's brow rose. "Jelena…"

"He is dead, and digging him up won't change that. But the wounds he received—" She pointed at the paper. "—they match this description. Anyone could see it wasn't wolves. But there was no better answer, so that's what it was."

"It would be something," Koja said. "Something… tangible."

"If the Despot did not send us out here to waste time," Cem said, "if he is any true kind of leader, he would strive to protect his people, no matter how low of breeding they may be."

Tahsin winced as he threw back the covers and swung his legs out over the bed. "Then we are in agreement? We exhume Teodor, check the wounds, and show the proof to Despot Branković."

"As plans go," Cem said, "it's the best we've had yet."

"So it is," Tahsin said, giving Jelena a smile which quickly faded at her tight expression.

"I don't know your customs," she said, "but disturbing a body laid to rest—on sacred ground nonetheless—is not a minor thing. It will require quite some convincing."

Koja let out a noise that may have been a chuckle, though beneath the mask it was difficult to tell. "Good thing we have a talented diplomat."

* * *

"You must understand," Tahsin whined, voice bouncing back at him from the great hall of the chapel, "this is not some flight of fancy!"

Father German, a tall abbot with even taller eyebrows fixed Tahsin with a flinty stare. "It is anything but. You—heathen that you are—come to this house of God and ask to disturb the eternal rest of one of his children?"

Things were not going well. In retrospect, it might have been a mistake to imply that *perhaps* some his group were considering converting to Christianity in order to get this meeting, but they'd been stonewalled up until that point.

"He is my brother," Jelena said evenly.

German gave her a pitying look. "And your kinship supersedes our Lord's?"

"Please—"

German let out a sigh, shaking his head. "Child, I am not heartless. I have lost members of my flock and members of my family. Dragging Teodor from the ground will not give you the peace you seek—it will be the opposite. You must let the dead rest. Give him that dignity."

Tahsin could feel the conversation slipping even further from his grasp and he did not want to entertain Cem's backup plan, which involved Tahsin, Vuk, a shovel, and the cover of night once again.

If he could just make the damned priest see, but the man was deaf to matters of the material and only concerned with the soul. Tahsin shot a glance at Jelena, licking his lips nervously. He wished he could speak with her before trying this, but he simply had to hope she would understand.

"Please," Tahsin said, bowing his head and mustering up his most placating tone. "I did not wish to speak of this in a holy place, but I fear not exhuming the body would be the far worse option. You are concerned with his soul, and I understand that—but do you not risk other souls by allowing something so tainted to remain in holy ground?"

Jelena lifted her head sharply and Tahsin quickly went on, having caught German's attention.

"It is not just his body that was mutilated we fear, but his very soul. If we believed there was any chance this was simply a beast, do you think we would be here?" Tahsin asked, nodding at Jelena. "As you said—dragging Teodor from the ground will not give her peace."

The priest's eyes narrowed. "And what makes you think his soul was... damaged?"

Tahsin shook his head. "Not just damaged—tainted. The same—" He gritted his teeth and forced himself to continue. "The same as her boy." He heard the intake of breath next to him, felt Jelena stiffen, though he dared not look at her. "Disappearing into the forest, day after day, coming back paler and weaker and *changed*. There is a devil out there toying with and killing God's children, and we must put a stop to it. The first step is to remove its taint from this holy place."

German didn't look fully convinced, though he had brought a hand to his crucifix , rubbing it absently as he turned his gaze to Jelena. "You believe this is the case? That your brother and son were… corrupted?"

The silence in the great hall stretched so long Tahsin thought she would never speak. When finally she did, the single word was so softly full of anguish, he felt his own throat close up in sympathy.

"Yes."

Chapter Ten

JELENA HAD ALL BUT RUN FROM THE CHAPEL after the Father German had given his approval to exhume Teodor. Tahsin had wanted to follow, wanted to explain, wanted to just sweep her up in his arms and give her what comfort he could, but he did none of those things.

Instead, he returned to the others alone and reported that they had permission to exhume the body and remove it from the grounds.

"Where is Jelena?" Koja asked.

"She… went home," Tahsin said slowly, then cleared the thickness from his throat. "It would do her no good to see the body again."

Cem snorted. "If I were so lucky to lose one of my brothers I might have him stuffed so I could see him every morning during breakfast and relish the peace of his silence."

"Show some respect!" Tahsin snarled, surprising himself by taking an angry step towards the man.

Cem didn't so much as flinch. "I show people as much respect as they have earned, which is why I speak to you the way I do."

Tahsin spat and turned away. "A priest will meet us at the cemetery in an hour. Gather your men. That's an order." Without waiting for a response, he left. There was something he had to do.

He found the door to Jelena's tavern locked. After knocking for a few minutes, he heard it unlatch, though it didn't open. He pushed it open and found Jelena already halfway across the dim room.

"Jelena!"

She stopped, her shoulders hunched, then turned, wiping at her cheeks. "What?"

"I…" Tahsin said, stepping closer and realizing—now, of all times—he had no idea what to say. "I'm sorry."

She let out a half-laugh, half-sob, shaking her head. "Whatever for? You've only tried to help me."

"I wanted—I didn't want to say those things," Tahsin said, coming even closer, until he was standing right in front of her. She lifted her chin to look at him as, on impulse, he took both her hands in his. "I just said what I had to get him to agree."

She let out a sad little hiccup of a laugh. "You lied to a man of God for me?"

Tahsin managed a smile. "Not my god."

"Ah," she said, nodding sagely. "And here I was about to praise you for the risk, though I see it was no hard thing for you."

"Well—"

She sniffled. "I'm only joking."

"Ah," he said, and there was silence after that. She turned her hands in his, rubbing a thumb across his skin absently.

"Do you… do you think what you said could be true?" Jelena asked. "Do you think…"

"No," Tahsin said, and he meant it, felt more conviction about that than just about anything he'd ever felt before. "Your ways… well, I don't know them all too well. But if your brother and your son died without evil in their hearts, did not seek it out, then how could they be judged harshly? And if they were anything like you, I know there was no evil in them."

Her hands tightened on his, and Tahsin felt he'd said the

wrong thing, then knew he had when she leaned forward and pressed her lips to his. They were gone before he could even protest, and he found himself staring at her face, cheeks still tear stained, though her smile was broad and genuine.

"Thank you," she said. "You had better get to the cemetery."

"I…" He was still holding her hands and imagined if he let go he might fall through the floor or float up through the ceiling, fully unmoored.

She let out a very girlish giggle, one that set his heart racing, and gently pried his fingers from hers, then patted his hand. "You'll come back after?"

Tahsin nodded. "Yes."

* * *

They had already begun digging when Tahsin arrived at the cemetery. The entire group was there. Koja and Arslan, a scarred retainer who nearly matched the other man in size, dug while Cem leaned against a tall tombstone looking bored. The remainder of his retinue lazed about a handcart, on top of which was the goat, looking pleased as ever to be on any piece of elevation that wasn't the ground. All was under the watchful eye of a priest, who stood slightly away, clutching his crucifix with white knuckles and muttering to himself.

"Decided to join us?" Cem asked as Tahsin approached and peered into the hole.

"I imagine my contribution has matched yours," Tahsin said. He had been diplomatic earlier and was damn well out of diplomacy for the day.

"I thought I might see what it's like to contribute as a Janissary," Cem said with a sniff. "It's why I'm standing around waiting for something to happen."

Tahsin rolled his eyes. "Koja?"

"Nearly there." Even as he said it, his shovel let out a *thunk* as it hit wood.

"Excuse me," the priest called, "excuse me! This is unacceptable!"

Tahsin turned. "What do you mean? Father German approved this."

The bald man thrust a bony finger past him. "Not that, *that*!"

Tahsin followed the finger to find the goat had pranced atop a tombstone and stood there, sniffing the air, its lead limp in Vuk's hand.

The priest was red-faced as he sputtered, finger shaking. "It's bad enough you heathens are here, even worse you have brought this barnyard animal into a holy place, but I will not stand by and watch it desecrate the graves of Christians!"

Tahsin lifted his hands in peace, ignoring the comment about heathens; maybe he did have some diplomacy left in him after all. "I'll take care of it."

He strode over and—with a little difficulty—manhandled the beast back into the wagon with Vuk. "Just keep her in the cart."

"Aye, I will. She's antsy here, like the last time."

Tahsin patted the goat, who nibbled his sleeve. "We'd all rather be elsewhere."

"Sure." Vuk nudged him with a shoulder. "At least he didn't see her pissin all over the grave behind the cart."

Tahsin laughed, then quieted at another glare from the priest.

Within ten minutes, the coffin was cleared and hauled from the grave. Koja dusted his hands, and then, without so much as a warning, pried off the lid. A foul stench emanated from within, enough that two dozen feet away the goat let out an irritated snort.

"God protect us," cried the priest, crossing himself, clutching his crucifix even tighter, and increasing the volume of his prayers from a murmur to something approaching a litany.

Tahsin approached, holding his nose and peered into the coffin alongside Koja and Cem, who had finally unglued himself from the tombstone and came ambling over.

"Merciful Allah," Tahsin whispered. The corpse was in excellent condition, considering it had been buried months ago, though it did stink. The neck was torn nearly all the way through, and some fingers had been chewed away. But that wasn't enough. "Cut the legs of his pants."

Koja slipped out a knife and did so, quickly slitting the dry fabric up to the man's thighs and peeling it away. The sight gave him and the rest pause, even though they'd expected it; dozens of human-shaped bites covered the legs, the pattern of teeth clear. Not only that, but they were child-sized. No sane man could look upon it and think a wolf had been at the body.

"This is what we needed," Tahsin breathed. "Get the coffin on the cart and—"

"Aaaaahhhhhhh!"

The goat's shriek cut through the still air of the cemetery, and Tahsin turned, standing in a rush as he saw a dozen armed soldiers in Branković colors approaching. He glanced at the priest, who looked just as surprised as the rest of them.

"What is the meaning of this?" the priest said, rushing over. "What are you doing here, tromping over holy ground armed for war?"

The lead soldier firmly moved the priest out of the way, striding past him, his men spreading out behind him in a semi-circle. He jabbed a finger at Tahsin. "You lot. Leave the body and come with us."

"Who are you to tell us what to do?" Cem sneered, before cursing at them in Turkish.

"Bring your dog to heel or I'll cut out his tongue," said the leader, drawing his sword.

"Oh dear," Vuk said, hopping down from the cart and tying the goat's lead to it.

The priest had collected himself and stomped back over,

hauling on the man's arm. "Put that away at once! How *dare* you draw steel in *urk—*"

His words ended in a wet grunt as said steel was rammed through his chest and out the back.

"Kill em all!" snarled the leader.

Tahsin took a step back, lifting his hands "Wait, wait—"

"No surviv—" The man's words were cut off as the head of Koja's axe buried itself in his chest, knocking him back into a tombstone with such force it cracked.

Tahsin cursed, stumbling away from the tide of soldiers and turning for the wagon. Koja stalked past him, wordless and resolute, his hands clenched into fists as Cem sauntered after him, sword drawn, the wicked gleam on the edge matching the smile on his face. Cem's retinue had all produced weapons, and even as Tahsin watched, Yilmaz loosed an arrow, seemingly right at him. It whipped past his ear before he could even duck and he heard a wet *chunk*, followed by the sound of a body dropping behind him.

He broke into an all-out run for the wagon. His arquebus was on his horse, not that having it in this melee would do him much good. There had to be a sword or something he could use, even a shovel! He didn't dare try to scoop one up from a fallen soldier with so many others around—and who knew if more were coming. They looked like Djuradj's men, though they hadn't announced themselves as such.

The sound of combat raged behind him—swords striking flesh, bodies hitting the ground, men screaming and dying and emptying their bowels, either the usual way, or through a jagged tear in the front. Tahsin chanced a glance over his shoulder.

Koja had a hand wrapped around a soldier's face as the man screamed, his helmet creaking and denting, until finally, with a horrible suddenness, it crumpled inward, sending a red sludge cascading down the man's front as he was dropped unceremoniously to the ground.

Cem's blade whirled in a dizzying pattern, parrying two assailants, his feet sure as he danced backwards, deftly hopping a squat tombstone without looking. One of his assailants stumbled, dropping his guard for only a heartbeat; his head dropped to the ground a moment later, and his partner's shocked expression only increased to find the tip of Cem's sword in his heart.

The men worked with the brutal efficiency of a group who'd done this more times than anyone cared to count anymore. Those outnumbered played for time while Yilmaz peppered arrow after arrow into the fray, making pincushions of the larger soldiers before they keeled over. Where Cem's men had the advantage, they wasted no time in pressing it, overpowering the soldiers apart from the rest, surrounding them, and putting them in the dirt.

By the time Tahsin came to his senses, it was all but over. His heart was in his throat, along with a healthy amount of bile. There were a few enemies still standing though. He turned back to the cart and felt an explosion of pain in his forehead, then found himself on the ground, staring up at the goat who hopped up on two legs and jerked its head at him as if to say, "Stay down."

"You little…"

"Tahsin!" Koja called, sounding alarmed. "Where are you?"

Tahsin scrambled to his feet, wiping a bit of blood from his forehead. "I'm alright."

"Thank God."

"Is there a god of cowards?" Cem asked, leaning down to a feebly struggling soldier and slitting his throat without so much as a glance. "I suppose you should thank him."

"I was—I was going for a weapon!" Tahsin said indignantly.

Koja halted beside him and reached for his head. "You are bleeding."

Tahsin slapped his hand away, suddenly furious, though

it irritated him further that he wasn't quite sure who it was directed at. "Find one to question?

Cem lifted his head even as he slit another throat, a look of surprise on his face, like he'd been caught dipping his hand in the halva bowl. "Eh?"

Tahsin looked across the cemetery, which suddenly felt very, very still. The only movement was Vuk attempting to work a stubby hatchet out of the face of a man who, Tahsin seemed to recall, had been moving, albeit feebly, only moments ago.

"Do you not think that perhaps we should have left one alive to question!?" Tahsin roared at no one in particular.

Cem stood, wordlessly, and crossed the distance between them, his sword still very much in his hand. "Do not test me, coward," he growled.

Tahsin drove a finger into Cem's breastplate. "You are the one testing me, you dumb bastard! I am in command. Since you and your men have seen fit to kill every single cursed last one of our attackers! It would seem the combat is over and we have now returned to diplomacy!"

He wasn't pleased with the way his voice rose in pitch nearly enough to match the shriek of the goat, but at least he'd taken a stand with the man, even if it might get him killed. Still, Koja stood nearby, arms folded, and though Cem could be an idiot, it seemed he wasn't that stupid.

Muttering, Cem produced a fine handkerchief, wiped the blood from his blade, then tossed the soiled fabric away. "I expect they were sent by Djuradj."

"Then for once we are in agreement!" Tahsin snapped. He wiped a hand over his mouth, looking around at the carnage. "Find the leader and—"

Vuk finally managed to tear his hatchet free in a spray of blood and teeth, stumbling at the sudden release and actually falling on his rump.

Tahsin felt a sudden wave of exhaustion flood over him.

"—and a few more who still have faces," he finished. "Put them on the cart along with Teodor's coffin." He blew out a long breath. "It's time to see Djuradj."

Chapter Eleven

TAHSIN WAS MORE THAN AWARE THAT, if Djuradj *had* sent these men, seeking him out at his country estate would be all but certain death. At this point, he was so tired, so furious with being belittled and attacked at every turn, he almost welcomed the thought of a simple execution.

The group, pushing a cart filled with bodies, one coffin, and on top of it, a goat, drew a lot of attention when they stopped at the gate of Djuradj's manor. Two dozen soldiers came rushing out of a barracks, weapons drawn.

Tahsin, with a growing lump on his forehead from where the goat had butted him, stood at the front of the cart, arms crossed, Koja and Cem flanking him, Cem's men bringing up the rear. They were all bloodstained, sweaty, and more than a few covered in dark cemetery dirt.

"What… in the name of God Almighty…" breathed the man in charge from behind the wrought iron bars of the gate. "What are you doing here?"

"I am Çavuş Tahsin Katabasis, sent by the exalted command of Sultan Murad Han, charged with the gathering of boys for the eternal service of the Sublime State. Despot Branković has tasked me and my men to find the beast that has been terrorizing these lands and the source of disappearing children. You will take us to him or face the wrath of two rulers."

Silence rang after his words, broken only by the sound of the clack of hooves as the goat adjusted her position on the coffin.

The leader stared, dumbfounded, before finally gesturing a young man over and whispering in his ear. The boy set off in a sprint for the manor. "We're just… checking on your story. You understand."

Tahsin felt some of the tension go out of him—some. If Djuradj *had* sent those men, the gates would surely be open and they'd have been hacked to death by now.

"We will wait," he said, mustering as much of an imperious tone as he could.

To his surprise, it did not take long. Djuradj—accompanied by a dozen more soldiers—came striding across the grounds, looking more intrigued than murderous, though Tahsin knew better than to assume by this point. He gestured for the gates to open, standing at the head of the formation.

"I see you've accomplished… something," Djuradj said, casting an eye over the group, his gaze lingering on a limp, uniformed arm hanging from the side of the cart. "I think now would be a good time for an explanation."

"We were attacked," Tahsin said. "In a cemetery nonetheless, and defended ourselves accordingly. The men wore Branković colors."

"So it seems, but they are not *my* men." Djuradj approached the cart, flanked closely by a half-dozen soldiers, who eyed Tahsin's group with outright hostility. "I believe this man was in the employ of my son, Stefan."

"That would make sense," Tahsin said.

Djuradj fixed him with a stare. "Would it now? Not to me." He flicked a finger and his soldiers spread out, half-surrounding the group. "I would like it to, though. I would like that very much, so please, go on."

Tahsin explained it all, even breaking into Stefan's laboratory. Djuradj listened intently, his look of outright skepticism slowly fading into deep concern, and genuine apprehension when Teodor's corpse was revealed and the bites made visible.

"This is… troubling," Djuradj said.

Tahsin opened his mouth to respond and stopped at the sound of galloping hoofbeats. The group spun as hands shot to weapons. A dozen armed riders raced down the road towards them.

"What in all that is holy?" said Djuradj, pushing past Tahsin to lift his hand. "Halt!"

The lead rider pulled his horse to a halt, dirty flying from its hooves. It was Stefan, the glow from beneath his blindfold visible even in the daylight.

"Father!" Stefan called as his men dismounted and drew their steel. "Step away from those heathens! They are dangerous. They just slaughtered a dozen of my men."

"Get down from that horse and you can join them," spat Cem, his blade already in hand.

"*Enough!*" boomed Djuradj. "If a drop of blood is spilled here, every single one of you—every single one—" He fixed Stefan with a deadly expression. "—will be drawn and quartered. Do I make myself clear?"

Stefan waved for his men to lower their weapons, though they did not sheathe them. Tahsin gave the same signal to his group.

"Stefan," Djuradj said. "I have been told some very disconcerting things."

"By the Turks father, and you know as well as I the lies they spew. You would believe them over your own son? The people who mutilated me?"

Djuradj shook his head. "It is difficult to deny what is in front of my own eyes, and what is see is not natural."

"Is divinity unnatural?" Stefan argued. "Is not striving to touch the divine the most natural thing for a man, at least one who is not a filthy heathen?"

"There is nothing divine in dealing with devils," Tahsin snapped.

"Devils," Stefan said. "Devils, says the Turk, says the man leading the brute who blinded me with a hot poker. I say the devils are among us. My sight is a gift from God. Why else would it be the cherubim who healed me? I reposed in their garden in the forest cave, and I was healed."

Djuradj's brow knitted. "Cherubim?"

"Yes, father. Angels. I can show them to you and you will see I tell nothing but the truth—God's truth."

"With respect," Tahsin said, "he has mistaken these creatures for something they are not. Would cherubim tear a man to shreds? Lure children into the forest, never to return? These creatures are evil."

"Lies, father. Lies."

"He has been—" Tahsin started.

"Silence," Djuradj said sharpy. "You have spoken your piece and I have heard you out. I will do no less for my own son."

Tahsin bit his tongue and bowed his head. After a tense stretch of deliberation, Djuradj spoke again, pointing at Stefan.

"You will lead us to the cherubim—all of us. We will see who is telling the truth and who is lying."

Stefan smiled. "Of course, father."

"We will be *very* outnumbered if both groups turn against us," Koja murmured.

"I don't think coming along is optional," Tahsin said out of the corner of his mouth, keeping a smile on his face even as his breakfast threatened to come up. He sidled around the cart. "Vuk."

"Aye?"

Tahsin looked up at the goat, who looked back with one slitted eye. "You said she got jumpy at the monastery, right?"

"She did."

"We know Stefan has been dealing with the fae—perhaps she could smell them."

Vuk shrugged. "Could be."

The goat took a few steps towards him, and Tahsin edged away, unwilling to chance another headbutt.

"Better bring her along."

* * *

They left the horses tied at the tree line and followed Stefan into the dense forest. Koja felt the air change as soon as the shadow of the canopy fell over him. It was so much cooler, quieter here, nothing like the city he grew up in. The quiet made him uneasy, though not as much as their situation.

Stefan had a dozen men, and his group took the lead. Djuradj had thrice that number, and they surrounded him, viewing Koja and the others with outright distrust. They were angry that their lord was being dragged into such a place and with such people.

Koja stuck close to Tahsin, who eyed the dark trees with visible fear. He kept his head held high, even as beads of nervous sweat formed on his brow despite the cool air. He was pleased Cem's men were with them. He'd been impressed with how well they fought at the cemetery, and if things went bad, they would need that expertise if things turned bad.

Even so, it would likely be pointless. If Djuradj and Stefan turned against them, they would die. It was as simple as that. Those who fled might stand a chance, or perhaps they'd be run down, or worse, killed by the fae.

Koja thought of the men and women he'd killed. He didn't remember their faces, since a face was hardly the most important part of someone trying to kill you. He remembered other things though. The sounds, which were similar, but never the same. The grunts of exertion, the gasps of pain, of shock, the gurgles of lungs full of blood. He remembered muscles under skin, the way they would shift and tense, even as an attacker remained still, telling him all he needed to know to expect the next blow. He remembered feet in the bloody sand, scraping, turning, preparing for a strike.

The coolness reminded him of waiting in the shadows before he was announced, of the chill he felt stepping back into the dark after, covered in blood and stinging sweat. It was never long before he was called again. He stood in the darkness, eyes fixed on that line in the sand, one side shadow, the other light.

In fact, he could hear the crowd chanting for him now.

* * *

Cem cursed as another gnarled root caught his boot, nearly sending him sprawling on his face. He hated the trees, hated the scratching bushes, the choking pollen. In fact, he didn't really care for plants at all. He had once, he thought, surprised at the memory. He remembered being very little, holding his mother's hand as she strolled through her garden, the plants higher than his head. He remembered stopping to stare at every butterfly, caterpillar, and ant that crawled up the stems, and remembered her stopping each time with him, never rushing him along.

Once she took him to a vast medicinal garden and he'd somehow wandered off. He remembered the moment of realization, the utter, paralyzing fear of being alone. Just the memory was enough to quicken his heart now, enough to leave a sour taste in his mouth.

Fear was weakness, and he was not weak. He was surrounded by weaklings though, from the townspeople so scared they looked for a wolf as the source of their problems, to this idiot Despot, too afraid to see his son for what he really was. And then there was Tahsin, perhaps the worst of them all, a disgusting excuse for a soldier, even amongst the worthless Janissaries he was nothing.

It shouldn't have surprised him that his words on ambition

had fallen on deaf ears. Did a dog have any ambition aside from licking its master's boots?

Cem had once had a dog. Well, it hadn't exactly been his. It was a scruffy little mongrel he'd found digging beneath the wall of his father's estate, a pitiful thing, all skin and bones and floppy ears. He'd snuck it some of his chicken and giggled as it licked his fingers clean, desperately, but ever so gently, cleaning every last spot of grease from them. He remembered its tail, like a little whip hitting his foot as it wagged and the piteous noise it made, cut off abruptly, as his father's boot had crushed its skull after finding him skipping out on his tutors to feed it.

Cem's lip curled at the thought of his father. There was perhaps no one he hated more in the world, though Tahsin was coming up on a close second. He found his hand on this hilt of his sword as he glared at the man's back. If he wanted to surpass his father—oh, and there was nothing, *nothing* more that Cem wanted—he could not afford to be associated with such worthless things.

He hated his father, but had to admit the man made a good point; if you keep feeding mongrels, they'll never stop coming around. Well, he'd fed Tahsin's boundless ego enough. It was time to end this charade, time to take the next step to becoming emperor. All he had to do was kill Tahsin. Honestly, he would do it even if it wouldn't help. When he became the most powerful, most feared, most respected ruler ever to have lived, he'd have a hundred dogs. Maybe even a thousand.

Cem drew his sword.

* * *

Tahsin found the quiet of the forest disconcerting. He'd never have thought he would miss his companions talking, considering it was mainly variations on what a worthless, cowardly leader he was, but the silence was worse.

76

It was also somewhat unnatural. Though the forest seemed welcoming in every other way—warm sunlight dappling his skin through the trees, the gentlest whisper of breeze, and the scent of wildflowers—there was no sound of life whatsoever, but that of the group. No birds, no buzz of insects or distant call of a deer, nothing.

It bothered him less than it should, he thought, though it did scratch at the back of his mind. Stefan had set a grueling pace, his feet plucking a perfect path through the rough terrain that none of the others could follow without considerable effort. Tahsin had lost sight of him a minute ago, lost sight of his whole group actually, though he imagined they were waiting just over the next rise.

When he got there, he found they were not. Panting, he craned his neck and looked around. Then he turned fully. The entire caravan had vanished. He stood there, completely alone, fear gripping his heart.

He relaxed when he saw Cem step from behind a tree, then felt an even worse jolt of fear at the sight of the sword in his hand.

"Cem?"

Cem said nothing. He approached, eyes shadowed by his helmet.

Tahsin backed away. "Cem! What's going on? Where is everyone?"

Tahsin recoiled in horror as Cem lifted his head—the man's eyes were milk white. He looked around, then shrugged. "I don't know. I don't care. I'll find them when you're dead."

"When I'm—hey!" Tahsin scrambled away as Cem drew closer, lazily swiping his sword through the air. "Have you lost your wits?"

"No, I've *gained* them. It's simple. I kill you, I become emperor." He lunged and Tahsin dove to the side, rolling across the mossy ground, his fingers digging deep into the soft loam.

"What are you talking about?" he shrieked. "That makes no sense!"

Cem threw his head back and laughed. "I wouldn't expect a worm like you to understand the complexities of political machinations. Now stand up, I don't want my blade to dull itself on the dirt when I skewer you."

Tahsin whipped a handful of dirt and moss into his face, then took off at a sprint. The forest was no longer quiet; it was now filled with the sounds of his own panted breath and Cem's bellow of all-consuming rage.

Chapter Twelve

TAHSIN LOOKED OUT THE WINDOW and smiled, shaking his head. Jelena wouldn't be happy when the children came inside covered in mud. He had half a mind to dunk them in the horse trough before letting them in, but he knew he didn't have the heart; they ran circles around him, and knew they could get away with it. Thankfully Jelena kept them in check.

She came up behind him now, circling his waist with her arms and peeking around his shoulder before letting out a groan at what she saw through the window. "You're cleaning that up."

"Woman's work, for a man who served as a Janissary?" Tahsin said.

She pinched his rear, making him jump. "Your soldiering days are long behind you."

And they were. Though Janissaries were forbidden from marrying, the Sultan had been so pleased with Tahsin's success, he'd allowed him to retire.

Tahsin turned, remaining in her embrace, and looked at her. Her face was red from working the oven and he brushed a strand of sweaty hair from her forehead.

She squirmed. "You're getting flour on me."

Tahsin kissed the smudge off her forehead. "There, gone."

She looked up at him, her brow knitting. "How did I become so blessed?"

"Considering you worship a man as god, it's a good question."

Jelena rolled her eyes, dropping her arms from his waist. "And I pray to him every day for the patience to put up with you, not to mention our children."

"Speaking of our children… they'll be outside for a while longer…" Tahsin pulled her close, pressing her body to his in a way that left no question of his thoughts.

"You devil!" Jelena said, slapping his chest playfully. "I have bread in the oven."

Tahsin grinned. "And?"

She chewed at her lip, then smiled and kissed him, whispering against his mouth. "You have ten minutes."

She took his hand and tugged him towards the bedroom. Tahsin followed, his heart full of love. This was where he belonged.

* * *

The arena was where Koja belonged. It was a cage, yes, but he was an animal, and animals belong in cages.

Aside from that, he was happiest when swinging an axe, popping a limb from a joint, or plunging his thumbs into a pair of eyeballs, feeling them pop like grapes and watching the jelly run down the cheeks. They'd stopped giving him breaks, but Koja didn't care. He felt invigorated, like he could fight forever. And why not? It was what he was good at, what he deserved.

The sand was growing difficult to stand in though. So much blood had been spilled it had the consistency of a silty riverbank, sucking at his feet and releasing them with soft *pops* with every step.

They must have removed the bodies, though he hadn't seen

them come. All the luckier for them, as in the state he was now, he'd take a swing at any who approached. There were no friends in the arena, no allies. No betrayers, no mothers who'd lied to his face and then carved a new and permanent truth onto it.

Thunk went his axe into a torso, slicing right through the arm that had been in the way. When he looked down, the arm wasn't there where it should have been.

No, there were no bodies, no severed limbs. Just blood.

* * *

Cem stalked the halls of his father's manor, irritated. He couldn't quite remember why he was irritated, though being in his father's house was quite reason enough. That hadn't been it though—at least, he thought it hadn't.

He let out a sigh, rubbing his temples. He was starting to feel more tired than irritated, which usually didn't happen until he'd been at his father's for an extended period of time. Of course, now that he thought of it, he wasn't quite sure how long he had been there. But, it stood to reason it had been a while, didn't it? Satisfied with the deduction, he let the thought drift away and headed out the main door. It was chill in here, and he figured some sunlight might do him well, even though Cem didn't care much for the stuff.

He pushed open the opulent double doors and walked through into the bright afternoon. The grounds were flawlessly manicured and seemed to stretch forever. A veritable army of gardeners and workers worked, keeping their heads respectfully lowered. They were hunched, barely moving. In fact, the only thing that did move was a lone white goat, which raised its head to look at him before resuming tugging the leaves off a bush with its long pink tongue.

"My son."

Cem couldn't help but tense as his father, Emre, the Sanjak

Bey of Thesselonika, stepped up alongside him to stare out at the grounds. Cem was intimidated by no man, though if he were to be intimidated by one, it might be his father. Even at his age, he was corded with muscle, with a thick, black beard and hair only showing the faintest streaks of gray.

"Hello, *Babam*."

"It is a sight, is it not?" Emre asked.

Cem stopped himself from sighing. His father used rhetorical questions the way a mugger used a blade, and if he were honest with himself, right about now he'd prefer the mugger. "Yes."

"Such perfection requires a strong hand," Emre said.

And there it was—the lesson. Always, always, the lesson.

Emre shook his head. "Isn't that what we tell ourselves? That we always must be strong?"

Cem gave him a sidelong stare. "Yes, *Babam*."

Emre clapped him on the shoulder. "It was not a test my boy, just the musings of an old man."

Cem stared at the hand on his shoulder. He could not remember a time his father had ever touched him, not accounting for smacks upside the head. "Are you…" His father did not drink, but Cem didn't quite know how else to explain his behavior. Had he begun smoking opium? But his eyes were lively, alight with…humor?

"Are you alright, Cem?" he asked. "You look so troubled of late. If you can't carry your burdens alone, let me—*urgh*."

Cem had pulled a dagger from his belt and driven it up under the man's ribcage, puncturing a lung. He gripped his hair, holding him there as bloody foam bubbled from his mouth. "Who are you?"

Emre—the man who *looked* like Emre—reached weakly for Cem's cheek with a blood-speckled hand. "My… boy," he croaked.

"Hardly," Cem said, and twisted the knife. "My father has never asked me how I feel, and if I were to admit any sort of weakness, he'd add to my burdens, not offer to shoulder them."

He dropped the body, and before it hit the ground, everything around him changed. He stood not on the steps of his father's estate, but in a cool, dark forest. On the ground in front of him, dagger still in its chest, was a pale, childlike figure, naked, with overlong limbs and a wide mouth filled with sharp teeth that twitched as the creature tried to draw in breath.

Cem blinked at it a few times and it blinked back, paper-thin eyelids over bulbous, jet-black eyes. It reached one trembling, long-fingered hand for the knife, and with a single swift movement Cem lifted his foot and stomped on the hilt, hearing a satisfying crack as the ribcage fractured. Blackish blood welled from the wound like a fountain, and the creature went still, its heart pierced.

Cem took the opportunity to look around. He was entirely alone and found he could not recall how long it had been since he had seen the others. He had a vague memory of chasing Tahsin, though where he'd gotten off to he had no clue. He heard a noise and whirled, his sword hissing from its sheath.

The goat stared back at him, a few leaves dangling from its mouth.

"Oh." He felt rather silly at being startled and considered it a blessing that nobody had been around to see it. He slid his sword back into the sheath and kneeled to retrieve his dagger.

"Aaaaahhhhhhh!"

The goat screamed the moment his fingers touched the hilt and he jumped, losing his balance and falling on his rump in the moss. He sighed, then yanked his knife out, wiped the black blood on the moss, and returned it to his belt.

He glanced over at the goat, narrowing his eyes. "You were in that vision. How?"

The goat leaned down and nibbled at a flower. Cem wasn't sure what he'd expected.

"Come on," he said, walking towards it.

The lead was still dangling from its neck. What had become of Vuk?

The goat scampered away, but only a short distance before turning back to stare at him with one of those horrible slitted eyes. He lunged for it, fell short, and came up spitting moss. The goat waited only a few feet away and bleated at him.

Cem got to his feet and put a hand to his brow, pinching the bridge of his nose. How had it come to this?

He managed to catch the lead by luring the goat in with a handful of leaves, then tied the rope tightly to his hand. Now that he had the beast, he was sure as hell not going to lose it. He could hear faint laughter nearby and drew his sword, stalking through the trees and keeping a close eye on the goat for any sign of distress, but she seemed perfectly happy to trot along beside him now, showing none of the skittishness she'd presented when he'd spend ten minutes trying to catch her and making an ass of himself.

As the sounds of laughter grew louder, the goat's ears began to twitch, and she tugged at the lead, reluctant to go any further.

"So there's more," Cem said. "Perfect. Don't you worry little one, you're safest with me. I'm ready for any—"

Cem rounded the tree and was struck dumb with the sight that awaited him. A broad field of wildflowers stretched before him, an ornate fountain in the center sending crystal clear water arcing through the sky to crash back down in a broad pool, deep enough to paddle in—and that's exactly what Yilmaz was doing, naked as the day he was born, chasing an equally naked woman, who laughed and scampered away, spraying water everywhere.

"Merciful Allah," Cem uttered.

Yilmaz wasn't the only one; all of his men, and many of the Despot's, frolicked in various stages of undress, chasing naked women—who, Cem realized with a start, all looked identical. Vuk lay on his stomach nearby, his hairy arse cheeks bare to the sun, feet kicked up as he sniffed a daisy.

"Vuk!" Cem called out.

The little man turned and waved, grinning widely. "Cem! Join us!"

"Are you mad!? And how dare you call me by my name!"

Vuk rolled over—much to Cem's dismay—and sat up, letting out a belly laugh and flinging the daisy at him. "Oh, don't be so serious!"

Cem reached for his sword, then paused, taking in the meadow once more. Were his men illusions, like his father, or trapped in one, like he had been? How could he tell? He looked to the goat, but she had shied behind his leg and was pointedly looking anywhere but the scene in the meadow.

He reached for his sword; he could always kill one or two of the soldiers and hope he got lucky. A few less of Stefan's lackey's would be no real loss. As the blade cleared leather, every head in the meadow snapped towards him as one. The goat let out a frightened bleat and tugged at her lead.

"Shit." He slid the blade back into the sheathe and the revelers returned to their prancing. It didn't seem wise to step into the center of this illusion with so many potential enemies—and somehow he felt it quite likely there was more than one harvester involved here.

He scanned the meadow again—there was no sign of Koja or Tahsin. If they were together, or better, trapped in their own illusions, perhaps he could get through to them.

"Come on," he said to the goat, backing away. "We need to find the others."

Chapter Thirteen

IT TOOK AN HOUR OF SEARCHING before Cem found it; a perfect replica of Jelena's tavern sitting in a clearing. Of course, he could hardly tell if the clearing was real or if he was about to walk off a cliff.

He let the goat go first, just to be safe. If it fell, he could snatch it back with the lead. The creature would hardly be happy about it, but he imagined it would be even less happy were he to fall and drag it with him to both their deaths.

Two Branković soldiers stood outside the door of the tavern. They eyed him as he approached and one held up a hand. "Halt there."

Cem did so. The goat didn't seem quite as nervous here, which he hoped meant there was only one of the creatures about.

"What business do you have here?" the soldier asked.

"Is Tahsin inside?" Cem asked. "I came to see him."

"He is, but—"

Tahsin poked his head out of the door, a broad smile on his face. "Cem! It's been ages!"

Cem could hardly believe the wave of relief that washed over him seeing the man. "Tahsin. Listen to me: you are in an illusion—"

Tahsin shook his head. "Stop, stop, come inside, rest

by the fire. You look like you've been through hell getting here."

Cem looked down at himself. His hair was tangled with sticks and leaves, his armor mud-stained and sporting green streaks of moss.

"Come! Oh—you'll have to leave your weapons at the door. Not my rule! Jelena insists. Might have something to do with how we met all those years ago," he chuckled. "You understand, don't you?"

"Years?"

"And it'll be more by the time you're in at this rate! Come on! We're about to have dinner. It's past time you met the children anyway. You can tell tales of our old soldiering days." He wagged a finger. "Nothing too scary, mind."

Cem took a step forward and the guards bristled, though Tahsin seemed not to notice. He lifted his hands in peace and unslung his sword and knife, laying them on the ground.

"The one in your boot too," said one of the guards.

Gritting his teeth, Cem complied.

"Come in, come in!" Tahsin said, gesturing him inside. "Bring the goat if you wish, just come in already!"

Cem followed him inside. The interior of the tavern looked just as he remembered it. The only difference was three small, shrieking children currently chasing each other around the room.

"Don't mind them," Tahsin said. "They'll wear themselves out soon enough. Come, come. Jelena!" he called.

She poked her head out of the back room and smiled. "Cem! I thought I heard you."

"Yes," Cem said slowly. "I was just passing through and wanted to come see you and meet the children."

That was why he was here, wasn't it? It didn't sound quite right. Something tugged at his hand—the lead, attached to the goat.

Jelena had said nothing about it, hadn't even glanced at the beast. Cem wrapped the lead around his palm, letting the leather dig into his skin until it hurt. She was false, as was this place. He considered throttling her then and there, but Tahsin would defend her with his life, not to mention the two guards outside.

Cem gritted his teeth—he would have to do this with words.

"Sit, sit," Tahsin said, pulling a chair out for him as Jelena sat a plate in front of him, along with a fork and a gleaming knife. "Please, you are our guest!"

They sat next to each other, across from him, and said a quick prayer. The food smelled amazing and it was all he could do to wait. He'd had a long day on the road traveling to see them and—

No—he hadn't. Cem shortened the lead until the goat stood right beside him, resting a hand on its head.

"Tahsin," he began, leaning forward, "I need to speak with you about something. It's… a rather important matter, so perhaps we should speak alone."

Tahsin lifted an eyebrow. "If it's important, all the more reason Jelena should hear it."

"What a good man I married."

"Married?" Cem said, unable to help himself.

"Why do you sound so shocked?" Tahsin asked. "You and Koja were there! Don't you remember?"

He did, of course—Tahsin in a crisp Janissary uniform, Jelena jeweled and veiled. Koja, dressed in finery, still wearing the mask, and himself, shedding a tear of happiness at his friend's good fortune.

Cem gritted his teeth. "You can't even get the details right," he snarled. "As if I would cry at a wedding! Or ever for that matter."

Jelena hid a smile. "That's right, we all pretend you didn't."

"Tahsin!" Cem snapped. "This is not real! You are trapped in an illusion and if you don't break free, you are going to die!"

Tahsin frowned, shooting Jelena a concerned look. "Cem, you know you are one of my oldest and best friends—"

"No I am not!" Cem shouted, banging a fist on the table and making his spoon and knife jump. "We don't even like each other! At all!"

"Then why are you here?" Jelena demanded. "Can you not just leave him in peace?"

Perhaps leaving was the better option. If the man was too stupid to see reason when it was right in front of him… Cem shook his head. That thought was not his own—well, it was close, admittedly, and perhaps a week ago it would have been. But as much as it pained him to admit it, he needed the man's help. He couldn't do this on his own.

"Do you see this goat?" Cem demanded.

Tahsin laughed. "Of course I do! I'm not quite sure why you've brought it to dinner."

"Do *you* see it?" he asked Jelena.

"Hmm?"

Cem poked the goat in the head drawing an irritated bleat. "The goat at your dinner table, woman! Do you see it?"

Tahsin frowned. "Cem, you are a treasured guest, but you are in my home and I will not have you yelling at my wife."

"Apologies," Cem said, gaining control of himself. He changed tactics. "Tahsin… are you happy here?"

He took Jelena's hand and smiled at her. "Happier than I ever thought possible."

"How was it possible?" Cem asked. "I mean, marriage is forbidden."

"God found a way," Jelena said, leaning over and giving Tahsin a peck on the cheek.

Tahsin chuckled. "The Sultan more like."

Cem drummed his fingers on the table, trying to ignore the food, which smelled even more enticing than before. With his other hand, he stroked the goat's head. "Yes, but does that sound like something the Sultan would do?"

A flicker of uncertainty crossed Tahsin's face. "Well, we succeeded in our mission and we were rewarded—"

"Tahsin," Cem said gently. "That is not something that happens."

His expression darkened. "I don't know what you want me to say; it did happen, and I am grateful for it."

"As am I," Jelena said. "Cem, must you bring your dark cloud to our table? Please, eat—drink for God's sake, you Muslims would be a lot happier if you did."

Cem bit his tongue—he could more than tell that he was not going to browbeat Tahsin out of this illusion. "Perhaps. You know what, yes, I will have a drink. Something strong."

Jelena's brow rose even as Tahsin's lowered. "Very well then," she said. "I'll grab something from behind the bar."

"Cem, what is this about?" Tahsin asked. "What point are you trying to make?"

"Does drinking alcohol sound like something I would do?"

"It does not," Tahsin admitted.

"And do I often travel around with livestock?"

"You do not?"

"Exactly," Cem said as Tahsin stared at him. "This is not real," he hissed.

"You are not real?"

"No, *I* am real. You are real. The rest is not."

"The goat isn't real?"

Cem balled his hand into a fist and sunk his teeth into a knuckle to keep from screaming. He slowly unclenched his jaw. "The goat is also real."

Tahsin threw his hands up. "I'm not following a word you are saying, old friend."

"I told you, we aren't friends," Cem said. "We are barely allies."

"And why would we not be friends?" Tahsin asked as Jelena returned with a cup of dark liquid. Cem looked at it, shrugged, then downed the whole thing. It was either an illusion, or fae poison, but they'd been uninterested in killing them yet, so he expected the former.

"Merciful Allah, I thought you were joking," Tahsin said.

Cem handed the empty cup to Jelena. "Another, please."

With a wary glance at her husband, she returned to the bar. Cem leaned forward, flicking a finger between himself and Tahsin. "We are not friends because I think you are weak. A coward."

"And I think you're a bit of a prick."

"You see?" Cem roared, louder than he'd intended. His head felt a little fuzzy. "My point exactly!"

A flicker of doubt crossed Tahsin's face. "You really are a prick, aren't you?"

"Yes!" Cem said. "Yes, I am."

"Arrogant—"

"Yes!"

"Rude."

"Yes, extremely!"

"Vain!"

"I—wait, do people say I'm vain?"

Tahsin gave him a pitying look that to Cem's immense dismay, cut him rather deeply.

"My point is," Cem said, "is that there is no world in which we get along."

"And yet you expect me to trust you when you say, what, that my entire life is a lie?"

"Not your entire life," Cem said. "Jelena is real. Not this one, not these children." He saw his words pained the man, but Tahsin didn't interrupt. "She is why we are here. Because these creatures—the ones who have us trapped in this illusion—killed her son and her brother. And they will kill more if you and I don't stop them."

"I don't believe you," Tahsin said, the edge in his voice the only thing keeping it from breaking.

"I understand why you want to stay," Cem said.

Tahsin scoffed. "You understand love?"

"It is not love that keeps you here. It is fear. It is easier to remain in a fantasy than to face the world in all its terror."

"I am a coward after all," Tahsin said bitterly. His eyes were wet.

"A coward and a hero feel the same fear," Cem said. "The only difference is what they do with it." He looked around the room. "Is this your ambition?"

A tear slipped from Tahsin's eye and he brushed it away. "Pathetic, is it?"

"It is… not for me," Cem said. "But it is an ambition. And I respect that. The only question is, can you claim it for yourself? Or are you too afraid to try?"

"Jelena," Tahsin said, turning as she returned with another cup of the black liquid. "Can you see that goat?"

"What's that dear?"

"Right there," Tahsin said, pointing. "Next to Cem."

Her eyes narrowed, and Cem caught a flicker of blackness in them. "Has he been filling your head with lies, dear?"

"Allah forgive me," Tahsin whispered, tears streaming from his eyes as he embraced her, burying his head in her shoulder. "I want to believe it is so."

The goat bleated in fear, and Cem caught a flash of razor-sharp teeth protruding from Jelena's lips as she lowered them to Tahsin's neck.

"Tahsin!" He sent his dinner knife clattering across the table into Tahsin's waiting hand where it was swiftly jammed into Jelena's chest.

A horrible shriek erupted from her and Cem clapped his hands over his ears, screwing his eyes shut in pain. When he opened them, he stood in the forest once again, the goat tugging hard at its lead.

Tahsin had fallen to his knees a short distance away from a pale, childlike creature, the knife still in its chest, black blood seeping from the wound. It whined, crawling away, and Tahsin got to his feet, looking like he meant to finish it off. Cem grabbed his shoulder, stopping him as the creature forced itself to its feet and loped into the bushes to disappear.

"Are you—"

Tahsin whirled, his eyes rimmed in red. "Why did you let it go?"

At that, Cem actually smiled. He'd spent his hours of wandering regretting killing his fae instead of just wounding it. In answer, he pointed at the trail of thick, dark blood the creature had left behind.

Tahsin's expression hardened. That was good; Cem expected there would be more bloodshed before the day was out.

"Koja?" Tahsin asked, wiping his nose roughly.

"I do not know," Cem said, retrieving his sword and knife before handing the latter to Tahsin.

"The others? Your men?"

"Trapped in the throes of sexual debauchery. I expect there are multiple fae present. The only smart choice is to press on and find their lair. Once I broke free from my illusion, it's seemed easier to spot them, though I imagine a man of lesser intellect might still fall prey."

Tahsin said nothing.

Cem lifted his hand, hesitating before clapping it on Tahsin's shoulder where it was immediately shrugged off. "You freed yourself. I did not pull you from that place."

Tahsin swallowed, then nodded.

"Come," Cem said brightly. "We've more monsters to kill."

And with that, he set off along the trail of blood, Tahsin following close behind. After a minute or two, he spoke.

"What did you see?" Tahsin asked.

"Hm? Oh. My father."

"How did you know it was an illusion?"

"He was kind."

Tahsin said nothing.

Cem heaved himself up over a moss-slicked rock and offered his hand to pull Tahsin up after him. "To be honest, when his body faded turned back into that creature, the first thing I felt was disappointment. The man is a real prick."

At that, Tahsin chuckled, then laughed, and before long, Cem found himself doing the same. He felt a little mad.

Chapter Fourteen

"You're mad!" Tahsin whispered.

"Do you have a better idea?" Cem growled back.

The trail of blood had led them to a cave, and, conveniently, to Koja. The only issue was that Koja stood, axe in hand in front of the cave, surrounded by a field butchered soldiers. The familiar glow of Stefan's blindfold shone from the eye sockets of his mask, each as bright as a lantern.

"I'm not sure which of us is more certain to die, me alone in a cave full of monsters, or you fighting Koja."

"The monsters are the size of a five-year-old child, and even I am confident in your ability to stick a knife in one of them a couple of times. And I am more than capable of holding my own against that brute."

"You think that's what those soldiers thought?" Tahsin shot back.

"I talked you out of an illusion," Cem said indignantly, tying off the goat's lead to a sturdy branch. "What makes you think I can't do the same with him?"

"Hoping for another miracle is hardly a plan."

Koja's head turned ever so slightly towards them and both men ducked back around the tree they were hiding behind. Cem stabbed a finger at Tahsin. "We have no other options. They are weak when outside their illusions. That body by the cave is carrying a black powder bag. Get inside to whatever nest there is, light a fuse, and get out."

"You make it sound so simple."

"Fine then! You fight the giant, and I'll go stab a bunch of scrawny fae."

Tahsin chanced another glance around the tree. Koja stood at the mouth of the cave, shoulders heaving. Sweat and blood soaked his clothes, but his footing was sure, as was his grip on the mighty axe. Whatever illusion he was in, he was in it deep.

"Are you a foot soldier or a Janissary?" Cem asked.

"Ya Allah," Tahsin muttered and Cem clapped a hand on his shoulder again. A supportive Cem was still perhaps the strangest thing he'd seen that day.

Cem stepped from behind the tree, spreading his arms. "Koja! We've been looking all over for you."

Koja's head snapped to him. Cem slid a hand behind his back and frantically gestured for Tahsin to move as he continued walking forward. "Tell me, did you kill all these men?"

Tahsin gulped, clutched his knife tighter, and circled through the trees towards the cave's entrance, keeping out of sight.

Koja charged, his footsteps shaking the ground and Tahsin went for the body, tearing the pack from his back. He caught one last glimpse of Cem before the giant's back obscured him, a mad smile on his face and his sword in his hand. Then he ducked into the dark mouth of the cave, the clang of steel on steel fading behind him.

* * *

This challenger was different—he didn't die immediately. The black-clad knight was fast, very fast. He seemed to float over the blood-soaked ground even as Koja sunk to the ankles in it. It made him slow, made the man hard to catch, and that made Koja angry.

The anger felt strange. He was a machine, and a simple one at that. You turned a crank, his arm went up, the axe came down. That was all there was to it. He didn't need anger to kill.

"Come now, I've seen you move faster than that," the knight said, circling behind him.

Koja swung the axe, releasing it with one hand and gripping the very base of the haft with the other, surprising the man with the sudden reach. Still, he ducked it, the head swishing through a few strands of his black hair and dislodging a twig.

He looked a strange sort for the arena, but then didn't it see all kinds? Just look at himself. A masked giant.

"Koja, what you're seeing is not real. You are in an illusion!"

Koja grunted. How stupid. The arena was the only real thing. He knew there was nothing after, and what could have possibly come before? If there had been anything at all, it was so long ago it made no difference.

The sun burned overhead, boiling the blood from the ground in a hissing steam, leaving the red dirt cracked and parched. Koja smiled, turned his foot in the dirt, testing it.

"If Tahsin can manage it, I'm certain you—"

Koja shot forward, taking the man completely by surprise with his speed. He didn't bother swinging the axe, instead grabbing for the knight's cloak as it swirled behind him. His fingers snagged the fabric, and he yanked, feeling the weight of the man come back with it, even as he lifted the axe to drive into his chest.

The cloak fell limp and the axe drove into nothing but fabric and dirt. The knight had twisted his sword arm, managed to slice the thing from his neck before it dragged him to his death. He stepped to the side as Koja did the same, each circling the other.

"I don't want to kill you, but I will if I have to."

Any trace of humor had left his voice. That suited Koja

just fine. There wasn't really anything funny about the arena. Around went the crank, and up and down went his arm, around and up and down and around and around and around.

This was all there was.

* * *

Tahsin crept through the cave, knife held firmly in front of him. To his surprise, once he passed the mouth, it was light enough to see. To his dismay, the light's source was a series of softly glowing vines that covered the ceiling and walls, all trailing deeper and deeper into the cave and seeming to pulse like a heartbeat. A much slower heartbeat than his, but a heartbeat nonetheless.

He had noticed a trail of blood on the ground, but no sign of the creatures, nor sign of any illusion. Unless the cave was the illusion. He should have asked Cem how the man figured it out, how the goat played into it, should have done anything but seethe and worry as they followed the creature.

He could still remember what Jelena's lips felt like on his.

Tahsin shook the thoughts away. He wasn't sure if they were his or if the fae were toying with him again. He felt the reassuring weight of the black powder in his pack. He'd light the fuse and run, just as Cem said. He didn't even have to face whatever awaited him at the end of this tunnel, he'd be in and out, gone in a moment.

He came to the end of the tunnel and stopped dead, jaw going slack and bowels going watery.

The tunnel opened into a massive space, well-lit by the strange glowing vines. They wound over the walls and up to the ceiling in a thick mass, stretching down to the floor where a grotesque, bulbous mound of flesh sat, as large as a wagon. It shivered and pulsed, the skin rippling with the impression of human faces, as if it contained a thousand people trying to chew their way out from within.

"Allah protect me…" he whispered.

Tahsin shook his head and unslung his pack. There was enough black powder in there to blow apart a house, but the creature was well over a hundred feet away. He would have to get closer—much closer. As he peered at it, he noticed something else—a man, kneeling in front of the monster. He hadn't noticed at first, because his pale flesh matched that of the creature, but there was no doubt it was Stefan.

"Stefan!" he hissed. There was no response.

Horrified, Tahsin realized there were vines sprouting from the man's skin, stretching to the creature and connecting them like some sick umbilical cord. He fought back a surge of bile, slung the pack over his back, and took a step forward.

He froze, arms pinwheeling as he nearly plummeted off a cliff. The wind howled, his heart pounding in his throat as he scrambled backwards, away from the drop. As soon as he did, he was back in the cave—it was just an illusion.

Swallowing, he tried again. This time, he stood on a battlefield, a cavalier charging him down. He could hear the shouts of the dying, feel his sweaty uniform weighing him down, merciful Allah, he could *smell* the horse.

Again, he tumbled backward, and again the illusion disappeared. The creature in the center of the chamber throbbed, and Stefan let out a weak groan.

He was still alive. Tahsin swung the pack over his back. He couldn't throw the pack that far after lighting the fuse, and if Djuradj was still alive, something told Tahsin he wouldn't take kindly to his son being blown to pieces.

Tahsin turned at a scraping sound, brandishing the knife. A harvester scampered away, hissing at him, its feet making a very human pitter-patter on the stone floor. He hadn't seen any blood, which meant there were more than just the wounded one in the cave with him.

He hoped Cem's part of the plan was going better than his.

Chapter Fifteen

CEM COULD ONLY HOPE Tahsin's part of the plan was going better than his.

The giant nearly had him when he'd unleashed his full speed, and nearly done it again a half-dozen times since. Cem bled from dozen wounds, and could barely see out of one eye after being clipped by the haft of the axe as Koja feinted a chop, only to reverse at the last moment.

He had to not only avoid the lightning-quick blows but also keep Koja on his left now—he was certain that letting the man out of his sight for even a second would mean his death. He had scored a few hits of his own, a deep gash across Koja's hip that bled freely, and a shallow stab to the shoulder that he seemed to ignore completely.

Cem had considered running, and—putting the shame of it aside—had discarded the idea simply because he didn't think he'd actually be able to outrun the man, nor lose him in the woods. He'd long since lost the ability to speak, needing every shred of air he could force into his burning lungs, so pleas to Koja's better nature were also out of the question.

The axe came at him again, just as fast as the first time, and he danced backward, readying for a counterattack. The angle was strange though, and he realized too late Koja had never intended to hit him with it at all—he'd used the flat of the blade to block Cem's vision, hiding the punch coming at his chest.

Some little noise of surprise left his mouth, followed rapidly by every shred of air he'd forced into his lungs as Koja's fist slammed into him, sending him flying. He bounced off a large tree, smashed through a medium-sized branch, and tumbled to a halt on his back, staring up at the sky and wondering how many ribs he'd just shattered. It was an odd thing to wonder considering what was about to happen to him, but he'd oft heard that when a man was about to die, his mind went to odd places.

He found himself staring at a slitted eye as the goat peered down at him. He reached up, scratched its chin, and actually found himself smiling. The little bastard had been a good ally. At the very least, unlike his other ally, it wasn't currently stomping through the underbrush to bury an axe in his chest.

With a shower of leaves, Koja emerged from the bushes, axe resting on his shoulder, ready for the chop. Cem opened his mouth to say something defiant, but at that moment the goat hopped up on his chest and all that came out was a wheeze and a little blood; now his lungs were well and truly empty.

* * *

Koja stared. He had seen many animals in the arena and had killed most of them—lions from Afrique, a tiger, a pair of crocodiles.

But in all his years, he had never seen a goat. It appeared from nowhere, just hopped up on the chest of the dark knight, who let out a pathetic little sound and feebly moved his arms about, but couldn't muster the strength to push the thing off.

Koja stared at the goat and the goat stared back. Then it screamed at him, a protracted, human-like noise.

"Aaaaahhhhhhh!"

Koja had never heard a goat make that noise before. How had it gotten in? Had someone in the crowd brought it? That made no sense. And now that he thought about it, the armor the knight wore was far too fine for the arena, even if it was covered in dirt and moss. None of it really made sense.

"Cem…" the man groaned, "…Demirci."

Didn't he know that name? Wasn't he Emre's son? And hadn't he escaped the arena *with* Emre?

The goat reared up on its hind legs and butted him right in the gash on his hip, which promptly gave out, landing him in the moss on his backside.

Why was there moss in the middle of the arena? Koja looked around and found himself in a forest, his head clearing. "Cem?"

The other man curled his fist and rapped it weakly against his chest. So it was him. Koja reached over and removed the goat, who protested loudly. He wrapped its lead around a nearby sapling.

"Tahsin… in cave," Cem croaked.

Koja pushed himself to his feet and immediately slumped back to the ground. He pressed a hand to the wound on his hip, which he realized was still bleeding quite badly and had been for some time, judging by the numbness in his fingers. He removed his belt and began wrapping it around his leg.

"He might be on his own."

* * *

Tahsin had tried a dozen times, and each time the illusions pushed him back, so real he simply could not force himself through. Stefan slumped on the floor, visibly weaker than before, though he still drew breath. The harvesters kept their distance, though he could hear the pitter-patter of their feet in the dark recesses of the cave and knew he was being watched.

How could he get to Stefan and plant the explosive if his eyes would just betray him?

He looked over his shoulder, praying to see Cem or Koja, but there was only the sickly glow of the vines, which grew ever brighter. They weren't coming—he had to do this himself.

He stepped forward and fell screaming through the air, the ground rushing at him until he reeled back, in the cave once more. His stomach twisted and he dropped to his knees, emptying it, screwing his eyes shut and screaming with frustration. He turned to the thing in the center of the cave, wiping his mouth. Stefan was fading fast. He had to do something. How had the man approached without being stopped by the illusions?

A thought struck him like a fist to the face. Stefan had come here before. Stefan, who wore a blindfold, Stefan, who could not see.

Tahsin scrambled to his feet and tore a strip of fabric from his shirt, then tied it around his eyes. He took a step forward, then another. Everything remained black. Tahsin sagged with relief, which vanished the moment he heard the approaching pitter-patter of bare, childlike feet. The harvesters were not going to just let him approach without a fight.

Tahsin took a breath, readied himself, and set off at a quick pace across the chamber. The footsteps circled him, drawing closer and he increased his speed, making for the dull thrumming that came from the thing attached to Stefan.

He cried out in pain as a sharp pair of tiny teeth dug into his calf. He swiped with the knife but the harvester had already darted away. He limped forward, straining his ears for the next attack, managing to slice one of the bastards and send it away squealing as it tried for his ankle.

The thrumming grew all-consuming. Tahsin nearly tripped over Stefan, dropping to his knees and shaking the man, who gave no response.

Tahsin took a breath, grasped one of the vines, and with a shout of "Ya Allah!" cut it.

Thick, lukewarm liquid poured from the severed vine and the thrum increased in power, a deep, rumbling vibration Tahsin could feel in his chest, in his teeth. The harvesters—Tahsin realized for the first time how many there were, and he did not like the number—screamed in pain and rage. He heard approaching footsteps and quickly sliced another vine, sending up another cacophony of screams and forcing the approaching harvester to retreat in pain.

Tahsin worked fast. He'd cut nearly a dozen vines when Stefan finally reacted, spasming in the widening pool of liquid.

"Stefan!" Tahsin called, as he blindly prepared the fuse, setting it in one of the containers of black powder.

He had practiced cutting and setting a fuse a thousand times blindfolded during Janissary training; this was no different. Well, it was a little different, what with the angry pitter-patter of feet, the wet slap of thrashing vines on the stone, and the ever-present thrumming vibration, at such a strength now he felt it might liquify his brain.

"Tahsin?" Stefan said weakly.

"I'm here—keep your blindfold on."

Stefan clutched at his side, then found his arm, his fingers digging in. "Don't leave me in the darkness. Please. I—I couldn't stand it anymore."

"I won't," Tahsin said. "Come, get to your feet." With great effort, he hauled Stefan upright and got his arm over his shoulder before orienting himself in what he thought was the appropriate direction.

Of course, if it wasn't, he'd likely be crushed or killed when the black powder bag blew. Taking a breath, he peeled up the blindfold and cracked one eye.

He saw the cavern, dimmer than before, the vines pulsing in rapid patterns. Throwing the blindfold aside, he turned around—he had in fact been facing the wrong way. Tahsin lit the fuse and, hauling a weak Stefan with him, made for the exit as all around them the harvesters howled and wailed, circling but refusing to approach.

They were perhaps halfway down the tunnel when the bag exploded with a deafening roar, shaking the cavern and sending a choking blast of foul-smelling dust past them. There was nothing to do but continue, so continue he did. Stefan was mumbling something, his feet dragging to the point Tahsin was nearly carrying him by the time he saw sunlight just around the next bend.

"It's dark," Stefan said weakly. "It's so dark." His blindfold was still affixed to his face, dirty and torn. There was no longer a glow.

With the last of his effort, Tahsin pulled him out of the cave and into the light, blinking at the bright sun that cut through the treetops. He shielded his eyes, waiting for them to adjust. He had done it. He had faced the illusions and beaten them. He lowered his hand.

He had not beaten the illusions after all it seemed, for what he saw made no sense whatsoever. People wandered into the clearing looking confused, most in various and alarming stages of undress and covering themselves as best they could. Yilmaz wore a quiver, his bow, and not a stitch else, while Vuk had on nothing but a crown of fresh daisies. Some of Djuradj's soldiers exited the trees, followed by Djuradj himself, who looked no less confused, and was missing a shirt, his chin and chest stained with berry juices. Cem and Koja emerged next, and it was unclear who supported the other, but both were in a bad state. The goat followed closely, lead trailing limp on the ground behind it.

No one spoke; everyone stared at each other.

Stefan's legs went out and Tahsin followed him to the ground. The last thing he heard was Djuradj shouting his son's name.

Chapter Sixteen

Tahsin, Cem, and Koja waited in a room in Ravanica Monastery, not exactly prisoners, but not exactly free to leave. A crutch leaned on the table next to Koja, and Cem had one arm in a sling, his chest heavily bandaged beneath a fine shirt, for once not wearing armor.

Somehow out of all of them, Tahsin was the least injured. It had been a week since he'd collapsed outside the cave, and they, along with Cem's men, had spent it convalescing at the monastery at the request of Djuradj.

A handsome young man, impeccably dressed, entered the room and nodded at the three of them. "Hello. My father is just on the way. He is visiting Stefan first. I wanted to extend my thanks to you for what you have done for us."

"Your… father?" Tahsin asked, rather stupidly he thought, but he hadn't done much thinking in the last week and might have forgotten how to do it.

"Despot Branković," the young man replied.

"You are not Grgur," Koja said, seemingly struck by the same affliction as Tahsin.

"No, I am not. I am Lazar." A frown marred his perfect face. "You were under the impression my father only had two sons."

"Yes," Cem said, seemingly entirely unburdened by the

affliction of the other two or any sense at all. "He never mentioned you."

"Ah. Well, there are some benefits to staying in the background." He bowed, surprisingly low. "Thank you all. Go with God." With that, he left.

The room was silent for a time before Cem spoke again. "Perhaps I shouldn't have said it exactly that way." Koja chuckled, and even Cem let out a short, rueful laugh before clutching his ribs with a wince.

The door opened and Djuradj swept inside, alone. That was a good sign. He carried a thick book, which he handed over to Tahsin, who took it with a questioning glance.

"Your ledger, as promised," Djuradj said. "Look it over as much as you wish. The boys will be sent immediately."

"Thank you," Tahsin said.

Djuradj nodded, pulling a chair out and sitting heavily. He looked like he hadn't slept in days. "Thank you for pulling Stefan from that place."

"Is he—"

Djuradj shook his head. "Still unconscious. It is in God's hands now, as I suppose all things are."

Tahsin bowed his head. "I will pray for his recovery."

"I would rather you find the man responsible and kill him," Djuradj said. "Cardinal Cesarini."

Tahsin frowned. "What?"

Djuradj spread his hands. "I am in a delicate position. I can hardly go to war with all of Christendom. I thought it would be a minor thing to allow a Cardinal to hide out in my lands, but I was mistaken. With what happened to Stefan, I fear greatly what other evils the man may unleash upon us— all of us, Muslim and Christian alike."

"So where is he?" Tahsin asked.

Djuradj's expression soured. "Stefan found him a place to set up shop. I didn't want to know. I'm afraid Stefan's men who might have known were killed by your man Koja outside the cave. Cesarini could be in any of a dozen abandoned towers or outposts. I can point you in the right direction, but I'm afraid that's all I can do."

Tahsin was surprised to find he believed the man. "Thank you."

"We will find him," Koja said. "And put a stop to his black magic."

Djuradj rose wearily and bowed his head. "May God watch over you."

* * *

Tahsin was scared. Sometimes it felt like that was his permanent state of being. Certainly it had been since this mission had started. The horses were loaded down with supplies, they had their next stop—a place called Kluv—and they were ready to leave. There was just one thing he had left to do, but he wasn't sure he had the strength.

He steeled himself and rapped his knuckles on the tavern door. It was the crack of dawn, and the street was entirely empty. The others waited around the corner.

A moment later, the door opened.

"Jel—*oof!*"

She slammed into him, wrapping her arms around him in a squeeze that took his breath away before quickly remembering herself and releasing him. "You're alright."

"I am."

"Thank God."

She looked past him to his horse and chewed at the side of her lip. "You're leaving."

Tahsin nodded slowly, unable to lift his gaze from the ground. "I am."

Memories played through his head, a stream of fragmented moments; the morning sun catching her hair, turning it to threads of gold, her laugh, bright and unabashed, her breath on his cheek, her lips on his ear, whispering words of love.

He knew the memories were false and therefore shouldn't make him hurt. Shouldn't make him feel anything at all, as insubstantial as any dream. He knew, just like any dream, they could never be fulfilled.

"Tahsin?"

But he was damn well going to try.

He took her hand and met her eyes, which looked as wet as his felt. "Do you want me to return?"

"Yes." There was no hesitation.

Tahsin leaned in and planted a hasty kiss on her lips. "Then I shall. I promise."

"Aaaaaaahhhhhh!"

Tahsin sprang away from her as if he'd been burned, though she did not release his hand. He turned, finding Cem and the goat standing there.

Cem stared at them, a stern expression on his face, and Tahsin readied himself for a lecture about how women were a distraction from soldiering, about how his single stolen kiss was a betrayal of the highest order.

Instead, Cem thrust the goat's lead at Jelena. "Here."

Jelena took the lead, giving Tahsin a quizzical look.

"Her name is Pickle," Cem said. "I will pass back through these lands someday, and when I do—"

"She will be fat and happy," Jelena said.

Cem gave her a curt nod and turned on his heel, crouching to scratch the goat under the chin. Then he rose and strode away without a backward glance.

Jelena's hand was still in Tahsin's, though now she slipped it free. Tahsin swallowed a lump in his throat.

"Give me your knife," she said.

He lifted a brow, but did so. Jelena took it, lifted it to her head, and cut free a lock of hair before Tahsin could protest.

She swiftly looped it, tied it with a bit of ribbon and pressed it into his hand, curling his fingers over it.

"Come back to me."

Tahsin nodded. "I will," he croaked. "I will," he repeated, clearer. He clutched the lock of hair tightly, palms sweating.

A smile played at Jelena's lips. "The sooner you leave, the sooner you'll return, no?"

"Heh. I suppose."

"Then away with you," she said, shooing him. "I have to find a place for this one and get to baking."

Tahsin nodded, then turned and strode for his horse. He'd made it nearly ten steps before he looked back and found her watching him with a faint smile, though she wiped at her cheek. Tahsin hoisted himself up on the horse, lifted his hand in a final wave, then rode off. He didn't look back for fear he would climb down and run to her.

He paused when he'd rounded the corner, wiped at his eyes, then his nose, then his eyes again. When he'd done what he could, he nudged his horse down the street to where the others waited.

"Are—" Tahsin coughed, covering the crack in his voice. "Are the men ready? We ride for Kluv."

"They are and have been for a while," Cem said, though he left it at that.

"Are you?" Koja asked.

Tahsin turned his horse, taking his place at the head of the column. The sun crept over the horizon, lighting the sky in brilliant reds and golds. He rubbed at the lock of Jelena's hair, then slipped it into his pocket, remembering its golden color in the morning light and promising himself he would see her like that again someday.

"Yes."